DIVINE IN ESSENCE
STORIES

BY

YARROW PAISLEY

Whisk(e)y Tit
VT & NYC

ABANDON ALL YE WHO ENTER

The sensorium is contemptuous of time. The limb you lost remains forever flexing, and the child you lost is always just behind you, silent and following. Absence is presence. None is all.

Meanwhile, the imaginarium entangles time. The pseudopods of the present insinuate into the past, blundering among the artfully arranged knick-knacks of Memory, knocking them aside to reveal the mirror behind.

A narrator speaks you through your life. You are a Word on the tongue of the world. Continuously, that Word recites your want, your thought, your love. The Word reveals you to yourself. The Word demonstrates your flesh to onlookers. The Word flogs you in public and soothes you with private caresses.

You have no power over the Word, no alternative: you must listen to the story it relentlessly and mercilessly tells. You must *suffer* it. Bow to your deepest angle.

And yet, when you sit down to intend a narrative of your own—a narrative not about you albeit entirely about you—that is when the Word goes silent.

Mouth agape, entranced, forgetful of purpose, the world begins to listen to your ravings. You become the cynosure of all consciousness. You become transparent to the eyebeams of eternity. *Suffering* transmutes to *ecstasy*.

Fool, your speaking was a pantomime. Not a peep of it

was yours. You always and only spoke the Word. Your body was the estate on which the Word built its Versailles. You wandered the Hall of Mirrors and saw yourself everywhere swelled up with delight, but when you tried to touch that lovely figure, you left not even a fingerprint on the glass.

What you took for the world's rapt attention was an illusion. That was simply your own gaze gazing. The world was not listening to you, but to itself all along. You were only the mouthpiece; the orator was the Word. Your ecstasy was just your suffering mispronounced.

AND YET—

If only I could stutter the Word. Just once. Shatter the Mirrors. Shutter the Hall. That would be magic. That would be alchemy. Transmutation. Resurrection.

Thou art advised.

TABLE OF CONTENTS

How more tidy had it been to have been born old and have aged into a child, brought finally to the brink, not of the grave, but of the womb; in our age bred up into infants searching for a womb to crawl into, not be made to walk loth the gingerly dust of death, but to find a moist, gill-flirted way.

—Djuna Barnes, *Nightwood*

God, I'm dying for it. How life begins.

—James Joyce, *Ulysses*

DIVINE

THE GREAT EVENT

Helen knew that something *special* lay in store for her. Precisely what it was thwarted her divination, but Helen in murky dreams had witnessed a stork nesting underneath the gallows, its bill opened wide to catch all that fell. She placed her palms together daily in eager yet nervous anticipation of some Great Event.

Mr. Runcible's opinion was that Helen required remediation *of a particular kind* and that he was both duty- and honor-bound to provide it. Small wonder she was never permitted out of the house.

Earlier in his life, Mr. Runcible had been wed to a woman of delicate sensibilities named Rhea, an often agitated and brittle woman who very nearly perished in the attempt to expel the infant Helen from her womb. On Mr. Runcible's conscience was the fact that some time later, he himself had caused her to perish in the attempt to carve her delightfully feminine body into a hundred tiny replicas of itself that he might distribute to every line of sight that existed in his house so that he should never miss a glimpse of her ethereal beauty, no matter the location of the room or the angle of his entrance, but as it happened, the human body comprises such stuff as does not lend to shaping. (He had, as have so many of History's finest gentleman, misled himself by interpreting literally the metaphor of "clay.") The pieces of his wife that he was left with—mostly bits of bone and gristle—he stored in the plumbing. She sustained the mineral content of the water after that, thus blessing those who partook of that house's cooking with rude and bountiful health for all the years it was inhabited.

When his wife's ghost commenced her haunting, she proceeded according to the tenets of a document that she had read when she was an impressionable adolescent. The text stated that "ghosts" were nothing more than waters and winds given voice and motive by mortal remains they touched in passing; thus, the necessity of burial in a sealed coffin, in order to avoid the risk of spiritual transmission to the elements. There was, of course, at all times a great deal of water passing by Rhea's bones in the pipes of the house… and, duty- and honor-bound, she confided herself eloquently to every drop-let of it. In fact, this property of the house's water contributed significantly to Mr. Runcible's aversion to washing his hands more than once a month.

Helen spent the idle hours available to her (and there were many) creating scenarios in her mind that were replete with projected details of the Great Event. Rhea, in her way, as-sisted: the knocking of the pipes inspired vivid and theatrical resonances in Helen's responsive, if whimsical, imagination; the susurrus of the flow they hosted whispered secret tidings of Historical sweep; and occasional eruptions from the drains augured of omens as to dangerous antagonists. From a family of birds that loitered frequently in the tree outside her win-dow, Helen learned of Rapture's dendritic profusion through-out Creation, ubiquitous in all Time and Space. Beneath the patina of Appearance lurked Truth, from whose bosom the Great Event would be launched.

Rhea's spectral duties were performed without complaint, and indeed, as a ghost, Mr. Runcible's wife proved far more agreeable on a day-to-day basis than she had done in life. She did not make of herself a nagging presence, nor a morose one—as appears to be the policy amongst a great many ghosts in the world—but rather punctuated the household narrative with a proper and appropriate set of inverted commas that truly could be faulted by no line editor worth his or her salt. The metaphor shall not cease there, in fact, for one might even say that an adequately punctilious Grammar of our Holy Life may not be assembled without the inclusion of symbols originated from the Other Side of the Great Divide.

Many hours constitute a day, and many days contribute to a month, and indeed the epicycles proliferate upon the cycles like so many barnacles upon the Ship of Eternity. As that most intrepid explorer of the Universe, Time, exhausted Himself across those hours and days and months, Helen, too, exhausted herself in confabulating scenes of some impending Great Event that she sensed loomed ever nearer. These scenarios were never as exciting as their initial inspirations promised. They lacked character... loveliness... color... moisture... grandeur. They were pitiably *insipid,* when it came right down to it, and Helen did sometimes succumb to a languor of wretched hopelessness and despair; but always, she rebounded from these psychical setbacks with renewed determination... until... one evening...

A torpor—more pervasive and peculiar than any lassitude heretofore endured—enmisted young Helen as she lay abed counting ceiling spackles,—a slumber gravid with implications of Destiny and History. It lasted full a fortnight, and she was fed during this period by the method of Mr. Runcible's chewing her food into a glutinous slurry and gently prising her lips apart so that he might deposit that proteinaceous mash directly from his tongue to hers.

With avidity, Mr. Runcible applied all the energies of his paternal devotion to the project of keeping vital the living fluids within the withering (and yet persistently transcendental and ethereal, in a manner inherited from his darling Rhea) *corpus* of his daughter. Her mother, he recognized, he had failed abysmally in this regard (attributable in the main, he believed, to the regrettably extended callowness of his Youth,—probably due in part to a poverty of poetry-reading during his impressionable adolescence, not to mention the near *absence* of swine in his childhood diet), and thus he felt keenly the obligation to succeed when it came to Helen.

When, finally, her eyelids fluttered open, ushering her forth into the dust-and-dry world from dewy dreams, Helen discovered Mr. Runcible standing in her closet, his naked body filling the narrow frame, his teeth chewing something behind closed lips.

"For the sake of our Savior," he intoned, after dramatically swallowing whatever it was he had been masticating (possibly bacon, as the room was permeated by that odor), "Who brought us the gift of knowing the color of Divine Blood, I implore you to erase from your memory the image of my enflamed manhood, to which your innocent eyes have been so shamefully... brutally... and *heretically*... exposed!"

Indeed, now that he had mentioned it, Helen noticed that Mr. Runcible featured an extraordinary situation between his thighs. And behold, the manly armadas! And alas—subsequently to the rousing clangor of engagement—the swiftly drooping morale...

Helen found within another fortnight that she was with child, or something similar. It—the child or similar thing—revolved and gurgled at all hours within her belly, never hesitating to protrude a foot or thorny fist whenever Helen thought a moment's peace had finally been achieved. It seemed that motherhood was as much a tribulation as her own mother had forever been warning her it would be (before that kind, harried woman crawled into a shiny new pipe that had been recently installed below the bathroom sink, a pipe which Helen had often thereafter found herself caressing and kissing at odd, secret hours of the day and night, when Mr. Runcible was out upon his rounds in the dingy, urban world that was forbidden to her innocent eyes).

She sought assistance from a bottle of Mission Wine she had discovered occupying its very own shelf in the pantry cupboard. The potent fumes aroused her propensity for dewy dreams. Her father discovered her drowsing across the sofa, the very bottle snuggled sideways in the pouch between her distended abdomen and her fattening thighs. Helen blinked into wakefulness to find Mr. Runcible on his hands and knees beside her, nibbling and gently licking at the cork, his body naked, his sailors sailing. Her neck carried two pulses, one for her and one for the... baby... but soon a third pulse chimed in, and Mr. Runcible could not contain his rage.

"Should I discover that your body is harboring an un-Godly *other*—or worse, multiples!—I shall proceed upon a lethal rampage that will leave all of you—*all of you*—gasping on the shore of Styx with no fare to take you further!"

Helen expanded in both girth and population. Upon the arrival of the third month of her Circumstances, it was clear that she contained more than a hundred "treasured guests" within her abdomen. Their limbs entwined and writhed in perpetual orgies, and while Helen felt at times that she was being excluded from a rather pleasant party, the fact that her own body hosted a space in which the ecstasy of others could be achieved lent her, she fancied, a status of sacrificial dignity. Unfortunately, Mr. Runcible's judgement of her status differed distinctly from hers, and the force of his opinion could be mitigated only when his manhood was enflamed and pig-meat plentiful upon his tastebuds.

Helen's innocent eyes beheld a slew of armadas, and Mr. Runcible found himself more and more wont to staying in to look after his innocent, motherless daughter, rather than embarking out upon those worldly expeditions that left her alone in the house to explore for Wine caches. Little Poochie, the doggy, would lap up the leavings of Mr. Runcible's shame.

In the night, it is true, while Helen slept, Mr. Runcible and Little Poochie held court together in the girl's closet.

And we see the light, finally! Trembling with fatigue, we swim for shore and leap out of the crimson waves onto an alabaster beach, unstained as yet by worldly corruption!

It was Little Poochie that greeted them first, his tongue lapping their tasty bodies with delight. Mr. Runcible's welcome proved less cheerful. As they writhed and murmured on the bed, clinging to the dewy body of their dreaming Mother—soapy froth bubbling forth from rubbing seams—Mr. Runcible unleashed all his fury. But the storm of his temper dissipated upon the swamp of their engorgement... Instead of torment, from his wrath, Helen's children were given the wrenching deliverance of *ecstasy*, an ecstasy more rapturous than any they had known before.

Mr. Runcible rushed from the closet in terror (Little

Poochie close on his heels, avid to slurp up every last discarded drop), and Helen awoke at once to behold her unGodly brood...

That, of course, was only the beginning.

Like joyous worms, the babies—or something similar—poked their snouts against their mother's flesh and nuzzled in the broth still flowing from her dewy dreams.

Mr. Runcible was not seen again, nor was Little Poochie. The gentleman resided, it was said, along with that forever romping pup, in a roominghouse somewhere in the industrial, northern section of the city, and demanded frequent deliveries (staunchly unrewarded by gratuities) from the local hamhocks shop (which was averred by rumor to double as a brothel on Saturdays and holidays).

"A life of free will may be lived in dreams or in despair," their mother advised her children before nodding off to death.

"Our life is a dream of despair!" they repeated happily.

Once they had exuberantly, but reverently, devoured their cherished mother's fleshly husk, the hundreds of her litter fell into a pleasing orgy, reminiscent of the blissful womb, and soon there was no telling one from the other... for their slippery bodies had congealed together into a fresh modality, perfect in form and divine in essence.

And from a primeval pool shared collectively across their networked brains—or something similar—an Idea emerged like an ancient hero from his bath, dripping and clean: *to make the world itself Their dream*, but not of *despair*, no, of *ecstasy*, thus perfecting existence for all who lived there.

Death, ah! that immitigable pestilence upon all mortal bodies once dreaded by the sentient Man became in one fell swoop a dream of ecstatic and unending joy! Once the world had been transformed into the pliant stuff of children's fancies, all the folk of History, on- and under-ground, threw off the yokes of labor and fended away the depredations of decay, grasping to themselves a new and, though strange, familiar mantle made of dream-stuff (admittedly still redolent of roasted swine and drunken navymen in pubs, but Mr. Runcible's influence on this newly recreated world was otherwise felt, at most, *subtly*, if at all).

That's, yes, how it all began.

It has not ended, either, it is true, or else your head would not possess the eyes to read these words... or, if you're listening to this account, your ears... but aspects of the story, heretofore, have not been public, and astonishment will soon addle your receptive brain, I wager, if you are a sensitive sort, which I know to be the case, as we are in this dream together, brothers and sisters!

Upon the unexpected (except, of course, by Helen, who all along had been predicting it), instantaneous rendering to perfection of the world into the dream of Helen's children (they all joined together in a perfect and eternal body assembled of themselves and glued by the Divine admixture of all Helen's bodies,—ethereal, material, chemical and atomic, topological (in spaces both Euclidean and non-), electrico-magnetomical, and (for the sake of comprehensiveness) not excluding inexistent), Rhea became freed from the house's plumbing to explore the limitlessness of Time and Space. Her preference was to remain in the pipes and continue to serenade her cherished daughter's living essence... but Helen was no longer available for haunting, being, in one sense, dead herself... and sadly, Helen's ghost could not join her mother, either, for the spiritual stuff of Helen indeed constituted one of the most critical ingredients of that cement that held her rapturous brood together in a body of such magnitude, divinity, and grace that *it could host a fever dream as expansive and eternal as the world itself...*

Thus, Rhea wandered through the newly made and deathless world, weeping, oh! continually (the hundred pieces of her dismembered body spread evenly around the globe, each bone and bit of gristle equipped with its own wailing mouth and tireless in its exercise), lonely as no other being in her daughter's spawn's Creation was, for only *she* was bereft of her beloved object—Helen, after all, had been consumed utterly in order to construct this eternal dream of life and death and all between—whereas all others, living and dead, were amicably corporeal and reunited with all those whom they loved and hated.

Years passed, however, and Rhea's misery proved catching, as the melancholy, yet melodious, music of her anatomically and globally multiplied desolation came to permeate the dream's prevailing mood, inspiring in the people of the world strange and dark musings... Romantic poetry... philosophy of Mind... theology of End... art in celebration of perversion and park-bench rants extolling decadent, indecent visions... Onanism in the bath... and of course, *more* music, often in a minor key, thus propagating even further on the face of our oneiric sphere a rampant cyclone of despair.

As the decades and centuries progressed upon the back of weary Time, and the dream of the world gradually descended from its initial state of ecstasy unto a lowly station of despair (in keeping with that advice that Helen's brood had received from her on their birthday), the ghosts of the world gathered in a grand hotel in Basel, Switzerland, for they sensed their moment was approaching. Rhea represented to them a sort of prophet of the dismal fate in store for sentient Man, although, herself, the Great Mother of All Weeping persisted unaware of their increasing adulation. She had nothing in her heart or sensations but longing for the lost daughter, who could not be found in flesh or spirit...

Secretly, the Society of Apparitions and Demoniacals (S.A.D.)—as the ghosts of the world nominated themselves during the First Order of Business at their great Alpine Convention—commenced a project to fulfill the Destiny of Man, which both their Idol (Rhea) and Progenitor (Helen) had augured in their separate fashions.

And that, *truly*, was the beginning of this new phase in which we find ourselves.

Divinity begins in Death!
There is no Dream that Death shall not Transform to Dust!
Ghost Life is Eternal Life!
Tombment is Eternal Triumph!

In these and other slogans now familiar to us, a new order of consciousness was promulgated across the world by advertising agencies and journalists of every stripe. People both alive and dead, weakened of their will and sapped of their joy by Rhea's perpetual haunting of all Time and Space, took comfort in the notion of divinity divorced from sorrow to be achieved beyond the dream of the world; and as their enthusiasm waned for the continued perfection of this dream, so too waned the dreamer's energy to persist in the dreaming of that perfection.

She had inspired the new decline, but Rhea did not know it. When her entreaties—no longer wailed into the Void, but now into a dense host of eager, perceptive minds that responded with alacrity and reverence to every gust that emanated from her raging, spectral throat—began to bear the fruit of worship and sacrificial ceremonies in the ancient vein, Rhea hardly knew what to do with these unexpected fumes arising from the fatty slabs laid out all at once upon the world's billion altars every week when Rheasday came around (and of course, in the bitterest winter month of Rhea, when the celebration of the Ides commenced with the slaughter and roasting of a virgin child elected to the coveted role by her superior resemblance to an old photograph of Helen that was reproduced in a particular painting, on display to this day in the Presidential Palace No. 53, located at the intersection of the Avenue of Justice and *Belle Rêve* Boulevard in New Hollywood, Amsterdam).

Just breathe, a Voice commanded.

With fear, but lacking will to resist—as no voice had ever, in this way, directly addressed her in all the millennia of her spiritual wandering—Rhea was conscripted to obey, and so she breathed.

Rhea's bones returned from the hundredfold branches of their ancient diaspora.

Therefore, we may say that the remaking of the world into the one we know today *truly began* with that precious, weak, and gurgling gasp. She choked and sputtered and coughed: blood spouted from the pores of every Helen-resembling girl in the world, and every Rhea-resembling mother fell down on her knees to swab her child clean with her apron. Rhea's wailing bones reassembled into a harmonizing body that was the world itself... and Helen's dreaming brood cried out in shock and ecstasy as it dreamed its own eternal dream becoming sutured to a skeleton of mortal sorrow... and its congregated flesh disbanded, the glue that bound the brood together dissolving to constituents, thus releasing Helen finally to her mother's loving, ghostly care, while the children scampered willy-nilly to the corners of the earth, carefree in their antics, hilarious in their laughter, not a whisper of the dream remembered even as they worshiped Rhea and her daughter Helen and gathered families to homestead on the perfect landscapes they had themselves, so long ago, Created in a dream.

I IN THE EYE

The first thing I noticed about my father's fiancée was not her glass eye, but the length of thigh revealed by the slit in her dress. Yes, she was the kind of woman who would wear a slinky dress to meet her boyfriend's seven-year old son.

The thigh was smooth and bare and firm and slender and moved provocatively behind the shifting isosceles window of the slit,—the sculptured, muscular outer portion revealed exquisitely in glimpses, the shadowed inner portion rendered irresistibly in my imagination. Thus, my first impression of the woman who would in time become my father's wife and murderer was that I desired her even though I hardly knew what "desire," *per se*, entailed.

She winked at me with her living eye, her expression saucy, and bent low to kiss me. Her name was "Clara—Clarabel," my father informed me—or did he say "Clara Belle"—as her fingers glided in to grip my scalp, rubbing gently there with force that drew my body toward her. Her dangling cleavage breathed heady perfume on me—a humid, dizzying, and pungent fog of aromas that engulfed my face and neck—and her lips were hectic on my forehead, burning a badge upon the skin that persisted in my sensation for days afterward. I experienced a kind of erection I had never known, one inspired by the presence of another person rather than the friction of my clothes or waking from a dream of noise and vortex.

It was then I saw her glass eye—perfect, dead, and blue. Its pupil was a scary centimeter in diameter, far too large. I felt as if it saw me, even unconnected to her brain; it perceived my face and figure and conveyed this image to her, remade into a dead doll, delivered alongside the living image captured by her living eye.

At this moment, my fevered boy's brain knew, there were now two of me: this boy that I was and this homunculus in her glass eye that was also me. If I looked closely enough, I felt, I might see it somberly gazing back at me through that pupil's portal.

I was not, however, at that time afforded an opportunity to look so closely, for she darted away from me and began to dance that wild bebop that overtook her in times of ecstatic expression, and my father joined her, laughing raucously, dancing in his comical, herky-jerky way... she made him happy... he was so happy.

My sad and alcoholic father's happiness was a strange, befuddling sight for me to see, having witnessed it so rarely in my short life. I was at once discomfited and pleased, afraid of Clara Belle for inspiring it and yet grateful to her for the same.

And within her glass eye, I knew, some little boy was watching, also, and possibly his evaluations differed in some degree from mine, but that boy was also *me*, and I was wary of these other thoughts I might have made but were opaque to my cognition.

After she had danced, Clara clapped her hands with declarations of my cuteness, which was "cherubic," then withdrew a disposable camera from her bag and aimed it at me, her living eye sparkling with delight and daring me to protest. I would not have had time to protest even did it occur to me; instead, I stared dumbly with an open mouth and lolling tongue at the gadget as its flash shrouded me in incandescence. I felt almost physically the laying of my shadow on the wall behind me at a strange, incongruous angle, and in my mind, even with the image still latent in the film's emulsion, I could see the photograph that would result: my open mouth, my lolling tongue... my eyes bereft of volition and intelligence... a disappointing photograph... I began to chastise myself. I picked up my marbles and retreated to the corner I'd been playing in before Clara's arrival. Clara and my father kissed each other lustily and commenced their evening's drinking.

It went this way for several weeks, Clara Belle appearing in the doorway, her svelte body garbed in clingy dresses, her camera occasionally foraying out to capture me into an image that resided patiently inside that plastic hull along with all its neighbors, her uncanny glass eye with its tiny, captive simulacrum of myself peering out at me... I could sometimes almost catch a glimpse of it, this little boy that was also me yet not alive, but the angle of her pose would shift or the lamplight prove too dim.

I knew my simulacrum must be in there, for there were movements... subtle gestures that appeared to occur deep within that miniature painted globe, which one might dismiss as incidental glints in the glass or reflections from a multitude of possible sources in the room, but which I knew more truly to derive from an imprisoned boy whose flesh was a doll's shell or perhaps even glass. And the time did come when my speculations were confirmed...

On that fateful day, Clara wore high heels that exhibited her faultless calves. She held out a thick envelope and smiled with girlish mischief. "It's you—I've got *you* in here, you cutie, do you want to see?" My eyes moved from her alabaster legs to her glass eye, in which I thought I discerned an oval, solemn face, and from there to the living eye, in which no face but flames and flying sparks I saw, and finally to the packet held so reverently between her hands. I nodded my assent, even as—too late—my belly screamed I did not wish *at all* to see what that paper flap concealed.

Too late, by seconds, too late that warning from my belly came. The pictures were already laid out on the table... the sagging jawline, the vapid stare, the tented shorts... a grinding noise commenced nearby... the light dimmed... and Clara Belle's glass globe of an Eye *turned*, even without muscles to effect its movement, on its own, *turned to look at me*, and within that Eye, a little boy faced out, a lifeless doll with thoughts that were *my* thoughts.

Yes, I finally saw into that Eye and confirmed the presence of my replica within it, but as I turned to look again at the photographs spread out on the table, I saw that they were farther from me than I had realized, and I saw that perhaps I was looking down at them from a higher perch than the one to which I was accustomed, and I saw that standing next to the table, staring placidly at the pictures, was a strange, lifeless doll of a boy who looked exactly like me... a simulacrum... except our places had reversed, and it was now *I* who was the simulacrum... inside the Eye, the glass eye which remains my prison to this day.

The boy who looked like me began to dance. He spun in circles, his sing-song voice emitting grunts and squeaks, muffled by the moveless lips, which were sculpted on his face in the manner of a doll. That smile, painted in the most lifelike hues, looked very much like my smile, but the eyes in which its pleasure sparkled were nothing like my eyes. Those eyes, like the one whose wide pupil provided me a window through which to peer into the scene, were made of glass, painted green to match precisely the shade of the living eyes on which they had been modeled. They expressed nothing but the cunning of their manufacturer.

Clara Belle took the boy's hand and partnered herself to his dancing. Together, they spun, and from her Eye, I stared down at the lifeless being who had taken my place in the world. I did not yet know what to think of him, and I wondered if he thought of me, or if he even knew that he wasn't actually me. I shouted out to him several times, but he ignored my cries, or at least, he gave no indication that he'd heard me. Clara Belle, however, heard me. Her giggles eagerly greeted every ejaculation. Her bebop gyrations intensified.

From the moment I was captured in the Eye, I never slept, never dreamed, never rested from my watchfulness. I, myself, became an Eye of sorts. I saw all that transpired from Clara Belle's point of view, and I became her internal companion, an unwilling but helpless Ear to receive her endless stream of witticisms and taunts... her monologues to me requiring no response, had I been at all inclined to provide one.

I found I could not speak, however, for infinite lethargy crushed my sinuses whenever I attempted to enunciate my mind's expressions. The more strenuously I essayed to communicate myself to her, the more torporous became the sensations of my body, as though immersed in glue. I could not sleep, true, but other forms of catatonia were not unavailable to me... Thus, I learned to keep my thoughts clear of judgment and cultivated an absence of emotionalism in my affect.

In this way, I maintained vigilance,—always, to the utmost, alert to any rumor of freedom, hopeful that an offhand gesture or comment witnessed at some unforeseen moment would enlighten me as to a method of escape from this impregnable enclosure.

Thus, I was able to attend from my vitreous redoubt every occurrence that transpired in the life of my family with a personal detachment that served to inoculate me from the spasms of terror and sorrow that most certainly, otherwise, would have accompanied my observation of certain happenings.

My "homuncule," as I took to calling him, loved to play with my collection of marbles (although I came to understand, grudgingly, that it was fair to call them "his" marbles, since if he had taken my place in the world, then he surely had assumed at least nominal ownership of all that had been mine). He would sit fondling the crystalline spheres for hours, rolling them about between his fingers, soothing himself with the gentle spectacle of those illuminated, cloudy vortices.

Sometimes, he spun the marbles about on the floor and watched their erratic gyrations avidly until they came to rest in some corner near a dust bunny... a series of siren-pitched giggles would hiccough from his throat as he chased them down.

He carried his precious marbles around in a little sack, which he tied to his belt and jostled purposely with every step; his approach, therefore, was always heralded by a clacking chorus.

Indeed, all forms of noise brought joy to the homuncule. A constant stream of chirps and grunts emitted from his throat, and he was often seen to be clapping his hands and dancing in circles. If music was playing, he attempted to match his movements to its rhythms, albeit unsuccessfully—

he was like a marionette under the control of a dilettante who never cares to advance his skills.

The homuncule didn't seem to mind this awkwardness, however, if he even noticed it, content with his simple delights and the frequent rewards of Clara Belle's giggles and embraces… she doted on him as if he were her own child. (Which, it occurs to me, perhaps he was, having gestated in her Eye… but who, then, was his father?) He responded to her attentions with great displays of pleasure and often crawled all over her on the couch as she writhed and giggled… or spent long hours lying motionless atop her as she rested, gazing as if mesmerized into her glass eye, although he did not appear to perceive me in there. It could be that I was not what he was looking for.

I sometimes wondered whether my homuncule's fascination with Clara Belle's Eye was not in some part motivated by its resemblance to his beloved marbles, indeed outclassing every marble in his sack.

Clara Belle took enormous pleasure in my captivity. When no one was around, she would dance before her mirror and caress her hips and breasts in taut, sultry poses, while from within her Eye, helpless not to, I observed and committed to memory every detail of the show.

She would wink at herself—or rather, possibly, at me— drawing close to the reflection, her eyelid shuttering the living eye and snapping open while her cheek assumed the contours of a smirk, and she'd say things like "Why don't you come up and see me sometime, you cutie?" or "Romeo! Romeo! Wherefore art thou, my little munchkin?"

At such times, with only an inch or two of air cushioning

glass from glass—the flat expanse of the mirror almost but not quite touching the convex surface of her Eye—I was able, occasionally, to glimpse the oval of my own pale face staring back at me from behind that translucent pupil. My features were placid and slack, expressionless, almost unrecognizable as mine, and my eyes appeared as nothing more than black discs embedded in a white mask.

Once, I put my hand up to this window at which I found myself eternally perched, but I was careful never to repeat the gesture, for in the mirror, I saw a boneless mass of flesh, in which the shapes of fingers could hardly be discerned from the protean jelly of my palm.

I persuaded myself that the distortions of the glass, both in the mirror and in the Eye, were responsible for this loss of distinction in my features, but I could not eliminate a sense of doubt, a feeling that perhaps the forms of my body were, in fact, gradually loosening into protoplasm to fill this otherwise insensate orb and endue it with a living humor... and perhaps *that*, to begin with, had been Clara's intention in holding me here.

Occasionally—one might even say ritualistically—she would retrieve an ancient book from the shelf in her closet, brushing away the dust and palpating the soft leather of its covers with her fingertips. She never opened it, only bent low to inhale its scents and smooth her cheeks along the wide, convex binding, whispering complicated incantations I could not interpret.

My homuncule's body was changeless—he remained always short, his face "cherubic," his smile fixed in place, like an image in a photograph. As the years counted out, my father made remarks from time to time, that his son's development toward manhood appeared to have become stunted, even halted altogether, at which remarks Clara Belle would take mock offense, saying "*Of course* my little cutie will be cute forever! What a treasure he is—better as a child than as a grown-up, don't you think?"

Over time, the homuncule developed a habit, when someone spoke to him, of vigorously massaging his eyes, as if wiping those glass surfaces to maintain their green and eerie sheen, and my father noticed this emergent motif in the behavior of the clockwork boy he believed to be his living son, mentioning it to Clara Belle on several occasions, but she soothed his concern with light kisses and bromides about puberty being on the way with all its attendant freakishness. "This is nothing, just wait till he starts panting after the girlies! Jerking off in his jersies, you know he will!" My father laughed and shuddered at such comments, which Clara Belle invariably coupled to playful punches and caresses, successfully diverting him from the subject at hand to more sensual topics that required no further exercise of language.

Despite occasionally observing such evidences, my father never noticed that his son was no longer a living boy. Perhaps his senses were too filled with Clara Belle's heady aromas and luscious limbs... which is to say, Bliss itself... a powerful inducement, indeed, to forget the causes of one's Suffering.

It had been my birth, after all, which drove my mother mad and into the arms of Easeful Death—a difficult scenario for any man to endure, much less a man of alcohol-weakened character as my father. It would be blithe and stupid to demand of such a man that he refrain from correlating cause and effect, merely for the sake of loving his son.

I do not say he didn't love me, no, do not misunderstand me, I say only that paternal affection (which he could not dismiss for trying) was not sufficient to compensate him for the tragedy my existence had engendered. For this reason, he had always cultivated a sternly enforced nonchalance in his attitude toward me, paying little heed to my activities and interests, even as he was careful to convey platitudes of his love at times he deemed appropriate for such expressions.

In spite of this indifference, and even though he could not detect that I had been replaced by a lifeless version of myself, my father could not help but observe that his son had *changed* in some degree, that the dancing boy with the fixed smile who was so devoted to Clara Belle was not the same withdrawn and somewhat sullen boy who had (perhaps in precognition of her perfidy) warily edged away and peered at her from a safe, respectful distance.

Clara Belle took care to keep the lights on whenever she seduced my father so that I might witness every detail of their "lovemaking," as they called it, as if love were a thing that could be "made."

They would dance together, Clara rubbing herself against his body like a cat, shucking her clothes as her bebop slowed to a languorous, hypnotic swaying of the hips and breasts, under whose spell my father inevitably fell into a trance. (Also in a trance, I occasionally noted, was my homuncule, who stood—seemingly unseen by them, yet making no effort to hide himself—in the doorway, clutching to his sack of marbles, uncharacteristically still and silent.)

Once my father was sufficiently defenseless to Clara Belle's beguilements, she aimed her Eye at his erection, which never failed to surge to full tumescence under the power of that glassy gaze. The pain of this monstrous swelling was so great that often he would weep under its duress and beg his wife for its relief.

Clara Belle's anointments, which were administered between her legs, only increased my father's suffering to such a degree that he would scream his unceasing agony into her ear until exhaustion overtook him and he collapsed atop her like an empty shirt, thereupon descending into fitful sleep as Clara continued to console him with indecipherable, whispered incantations, as if injecting them directly into his dreams.

(I wonder if he ever dreamt of me... his son, not the crude homunculus who passed for me... or perhaps my mother, so long gone from this world... or perhaps... perhaps, a useless question.)

Although, at first, the burden of my father's sadness was lightened by his association with Clara Belle and thus the vigor of his natural recourse to drink diminished; yet, after a few years, his alcoholism began to regain its former ascendancy in the composition of his character.

I saw everything that transpired in my household from my perch in Clara's Eye, but there were things I yet could not see, even though they should have been obvious to any onlooker. For example, I was never able to perceive the thing that brought my father low. He had been a sad man before his marriage, true, but he had been a happy man after his marriage... until his sadness *returned*... from what cause I failed to discern, despite devoting much consideration to the subject. There was no apparent reason for it, but he took to drinking more and more, and consequently, his goodness faded.

Whereas in the past he had been prone to alcohol's stupors, my father now was given to its angers. He flew into rages at the slightest provocation and even struck Clara Belle from time to time. With his open palm, he'd swipe her face... or with his knuckles, he'd hammer her kidney—one, two— quick, hard clouts—accompanied always by a grunt of pain— not her grunt but *his*, as if, absurdly, he had not bestowed but received the blows.

Without fail, my father wept and made amends in the aftermath of such scenes, and Clara Belle made as if to accept his atonements, but her rants and litanies of his offenses rang in my ears day after day.

"You'd think a woman would be good enough for him," she'd say, "A real woman with a real bod on her!"

Or she'd say, "Drinking's *fun*, supposed to be *fun*, whatever happened to *fun*?"

Or she'd say, "You know me, you little munchkin, I was made for loving, not for punching... and a *boy* watching the whole thing, his own boy, you'd think a father'd at least put some shame on and cover up that pathetic act of his." (I wasn't sure to which boy she referred, the living boy inside her glass eye or the lifeless effigy squealing behind the couch... or perhaps, in some metaphysical mode, both of us.)

Clara Belle stopped drinking altogether, and she demanded that my father stop as well. She issued ultimatums,—for example, denying those sensual favors, which he yet craved, unless his breath were free of fumes; she occasionally begged and whined; she even tried weeping (after practicing for hours in front of the mirror to hone her delivery to its sharpest effect, which she adjudged to require a subtle combination of sultry self-caresses and cosmetics running in tandem with her tears to delineate their tracks upon her skin).

My father would eagerly promise to stop drinking, but then he'd arrive home from work the very next day clutching under his arm a brown paper bag, inevitably twisted at the top around a narrow neck, his shoulders hunched in defeat and an apologetic, yet vaguely defiant, expression on his face.

A time came when she declared, "I'm sorry, cutie-pie, that it had to come to this, but it's *his* fault—*it's his fault*—remember that. Whatever happens, he did it to himself!" And she retrieved her ancient book from its alcove in her closet, reflexively dusted it off, and for the first time since I had begun living in her Eye, opened it.

A small compartment was hollowed out in the pages, containing assorted trinkets, gems, lockets, and beribboned bundles of yellowed papers. Of these items, Clara Belle selected three tiny vials and brought them to her vanity. In a crystal measuring cup, she carefully allotted a drop from each vial and held the glass to the light, allowing me to examine the mixture of its potent contents. "His choice," she murmured in a conspiring tone she usually reserved for the act of seduction. "Not mine... his."

She next went to the kitchen and removed from the cupboard my father's two bottles of bourbon. Into each, she administered a minuscule droplet of her potion and then submitted the bottles to a gentle agitation before replacing them on the shelf. "He can do the right thing or not, it's out of my hands. Remember that, cutie, it's up to him..."

That evening, before my father retrieved his bourbon, Clara Belle—garbed in her "slinkiest number," as she called it—proceeded to "pull out the stops." She danced, she sang, and she dropped herself to her knees before him. "Not one more drink," she said, "It's poison, do you hear me? I'm your wife, not that bottle. And that's your son over there." She pointed to my homuncule, who was jumping up and down, his green glass eyes glinting eerily in the yellow lamplight. "Not one more drink."

My father peered sorrowfully down at her, then stared at the boy who was not his son, and he shook his head slowly. "Tomorrow, Clara—I'm going to have one more night of it, and then tomorrow morning it all goes down the drain... one more night... that's all I need."

"He made his choice," Clara Belle said as my father fumbled in the cupboard for his bottles. "I didn't do it, he did. I tried to stop him, didn't I? I told him exactly what he was in for... I tried to save him from himself... his choice, his choice."

On the night of my father's funeral and her own last night among the living, Clara Belle brought my homuncule into her bed. "I can't be alone," she said, "I need my little guy tonight, okay?" The homuncule, his marbles resounding in their sack, danced clumsily around her, reaching upward occasionally to smear his cool, porcelain hands around her hips and stomach.

She had wept in front of the bathroom mirror that morning, and she wept again upon returning home from the graveyard, sinking to her haunches and gripping at the couch cushions to steady both her wracking torso and her rolling head,—but during the funeral itself, she had maintained full possession of her faculties, even inspiring whispers relevant to her "coldness" from some members of my father's clan. I was surprised neither by her public aloofness nor her private histrionics, for I had witnessed, over the course of the several years I'd spent inside the Eye, a broad and supple range of her emotional evocations. She was a truly gifted performer.

On this night, she clothed herself in my father's favorite teddy, a pitch-black piece of flimsy silk. She dressed my homuncule in his cotton, polka-dot pajamas and tucked him in beside her. Her hands moved all around his body, even slipping in beneath the cloth of his pajamas, communicating warmth to his cool, dead limbs. The homuncule made cooing noises as she kissed his forehead and snuggled him gently against her shoulder.

Strangely, at this time, I found myself subject to the first bout of sleep I had experienced since entering the Eye. Without precedent, my vision dimmed and my consciousness fled. I rallied to retain my senses, for I urgently wished to see what disposition Clara Belle had in store for my homuncule, but I was not equal to the struggle...

If I drifted into dreams, I do not remember, but when I came awake, I found myself in darkness,—however, not in silence, for I heard the familiar chirps and grunts of my homuncule, that lifeless boy who looks like me but is not me, whose thoughts I do not know but are, nevertheless, my thoughts.

Then his bloody hand dropped away from his face, and I saw him in the mirror: one eye green, the other blue—a distinguished, if disconcerting, effect.

YOUR MOTHER LOVES YOU

That first night, the door was closed, but I felt my mother's presence on the other side. I remember this sensation distinctly, feeling her even though I couldn't see or hear. I didn't dare open the door, but she stayed out there for over an hour. I was five, so maybe it wasn't that long, but it felt like forever.

The second night, the door was ajar, just a bit, and I could make out her form through the crack. She faced away from me, naked, her buttocks quivering, her shoulders slumped. The night light put its green on her. Her arms hung limply, but her fingers frantically pressed against her outer thighs in some pattern, jiggling her cellulite. I pulled my blankets over my head, and soon enough I was asleep.

The third night, I awoke to an odd sensation—my mother chewing on my ear. Her arms were wrapped around me, pulling me in, her teeth nibbling, tongue licking through the folds. She grunted and murmured wetly as she chewed. A hectic cackle, occasionally. It wasn't entirely unpleasant.

This was when I was a boy.

I'm sure you've heard about it; the case was famous, how she cut me, how she ate... And the doctors, innovative bunch, suggested I become a girl, my manhood so hopelessly foreclosed. You'd never guess it, to look at me. I'm every bit the looker, even at forty-three. Don't you think?

But a lot happened between those first somewhat frightening nights and the last one before she went away forever. It wasn't until I was six that I became a girl. It was the good part of a year my mother spent outside my door... sometimes in my bed. No, no, not for sex, not for pleasure, no, this was not a molestation.

Something commanded her.

She would mutter to it. "Is this what you want? How do I do it?" I never heard its replies, but I sensed the tension in her body as she listened. She was coiled inside.

Her muscles were so hard and lithe. Not like her muscles in the daytime. She couldn't remember what happened at night once the sun was risen and her body was soft like bunnies. Her embrace in the morning never failed to warm me giggly.

At night, however, her body was so cold I shivered when she hugged me. Sometimes, she had the knife with her. That, too, was cold. She would press the flat of it against my back or inner thigh. So immitigably cold, it was.

I was given its edge only a few times. Once by mistake, but usually at the behest of someone else whose voice I could not hear, whom only my mother saw or heard. "Is this the way? How will you be happy?" And of course, there was that final cut, the one that made me "Jenna." I chose "Jenna." They let me choose my name.

I strained to hear what she could hear so easily. I asked her for translations, but she ignored me. And in the daytime, such questions only puzzled her. And worried her. She thought I might be disturbed. She took me to several therapists, but I clammed up with them, I knew better than to speak of certain things. Call me a wise child.

Already lacking a father and with my mother gone away, I became my Grammy's ward. That whole first year, she called me "Jon." I begged for "Jenna," but she would not condone it. Or rather, her tears would not condone it.

The children at school, however, were easier to persuade. For one thing, they were different children, since Grammy lived in another town. For another, my eyes were bewitching. A few of my peers came under my suasion and formed a circle round me. I could count on them to protect "Jenna" from incursions.

All through growing up, I felt an emptiness within me.

I forgot my boyhood, even Grammy forgot. It is easier to forget atrocities whose aftermath is not fierce but gentle. My body was the gentle body of a little girl. Not fierce at all. My eyes were bewitching. My friends soothed me with endless petting, they could not restrain themselves from caressing me. The strange shape of my femininity, the softness of my gentle body—it drew them in.

They would whisper to me. "Jenna, Jenna, you're so sweet. Is this the way? How will you be happy?" I did not know the answer, not then, but I would place my head in their laps by way of encouragement.

My high school and college years passed in a similar vein, except instead of children, there were young men. My bewitching eyes would draw them in. They would place their hardness in me and whimper out their pleas. "Is this what you want? How do I do it?" I did not know the answer, still, but I would hold their thrashing bodies close by way of encouragement. I would chew their ears and murmur wetly as they came inside me, an excitement they almost couldn't bear but for which they praised me in the gentleness of aftermath.

I felt an emptiness within me, most poignantly at every birthday. Every year, I placed six candles on my cake. I let the candles burn to nibs since I had no wishes that I knew of. The wax would pool upon the frosting, cooling to a hardness, and

I did not scrape it off but ate as if to fill the emptiness within me. Only a symbolic filling, of course. I did not know what would fill that emptiness until the age of thirty-three.

That's how old I was when my Grammy died, and I was with her at the moment of her expiration. Her last words to me were a whisper I had to bend close to hear. "Jon, Jon, your mother loves you."

I had not, in proper, forgotten "Jon," but in practice, I'd purged him long ago from my daily thoughts… now the memory returned in full. The tears I shed on my Grammy's withered face were not for her but for the revelation. Not the revelation of my past but the revelation of my future.

I finally knew what would fill my emptiness.

And so I regret nothing. How could I regret? Were I still "Jon," then there would be no "Eli," or at least, he would have a different name and call a different woman "Mommy." I'll never forget the first time I held him in my arms. He was only one month old, still wrinkly, premature—that whole first month he'd spent in ICU. His eyes were closed, my tears fell on his cheeks, and he stirred… His breath was just a feather's wake. I held my cheek above it to reassure myself that it was there…

No, I cannot regret events along the path that led to Eli. My Eli now is six himself. A happy boy, he makes me happy.

Sometimes, in my dreams, I am standing in a darkened hallway. A woman stands before me, green as a corpse, her eyes round and terrified. Tears stream down her cheeks.

But she is dreaming, too, isn't she?

In these dreams, I stand before this woman, speaking words to her that are in a language neither of us can understand. Awkwardly, she strains to obey, but gets it wrong, gets it wrong! I'll do it, yes, in one of these dreams, I'll make her get it right.

She always pleads with me so piteously, but I am implacable. I am a sort of Goddess in these dreams. My bearing is grand. My body is sleek and feminine, so gentle, so commanding.

IN

THE METAPHOR OF THE LAKES

First Day

Evening... I am very excited to begin a diary! I found it underneath an old Fireman's Hat in the attic, its pages yellowed but *blank* and therefore most receptive to the "elaboration of my thoughts," I think—to use a phrase I've heard Mr. Menders employ—and I have spent all of yesterday and most of today in search of a pencil. Finally, I have one, and there are three more where it came from. Since I don't know what day it is, I'll begin as if today were the first of all days, the so-called "past" being mere background, murky and inessential to matters at hand.

To be clear from the outset because I believe in *honesty*, I am no longer certain whether I am living or dead; I seem to have lost track. Having spent so many spans inside this house, it is difficult to know anymore whether the outside world is forbidden me because of my "agoraphobia" or because I am a ghost fated to haunt only these rooms. There is little doubt at all, however, that I am a girl, a very *pretty* girl, although I can't remember what I look like... and even though there are things called "mirrors," in which one might verify an aesthetical impression, I have not encountered one of those in this house. At least, I don't believe I have.

My brother, whose name, for now, I must withhold, possibly because I can't remember it, is definitely alive. I'm almost certain he is not a ghost. I have seen him *eating* things, not just dust devils and stray tacks, but *real broccoli*, the kind that is grown in a garden and reaped and brought in by someone whose job it is to secure vegetables for repast. I'm not certain who that person might be; it can't be Mr. Menders or Mr. Scatt because they would be offended by any expectation on your part or my brother's or mine that they should perform a useful service even on their own behalf. (This is not to condemn them, only descriptive. Should Mr. Scatt chance upon this diary, I hope he will understand that. By the bye, do you happen to know my name, Mr. Scatt? I would most appreciate your information, perhaps you could write it in the margin for me?) I don't think I have seen any person in this house, other than Mr. Menders and Mr. Scatt and my brother (who is either my older brother or my younger brother), in all the time I've lived here, which is a very long time. There are *days, weeks, months*, and *years* in time, I know that much, and each of these measures may be applied in some magnitude to the spans I've traversed in these lodgings. It is possible I was born here, and if I'm a ghost, I suppose I must have died here, too... which amounts to pretty much the same thing, perhaps.

But as I was saying, *someone* brings the vegetables, and Mr. Menders and Mr. Scatt dine on them—uncooked, it must be said. Mr. Scatt prefers the "Natural State," and Mr. Menders disdains to quibble. He has much weightier matters in his mind to consider. He is a very intelligent man. His mind is in his head, in fact, which is where Leonardo da Vinci kept his, and we all know how intelligent that man was. *Very.*

My brother eats the vegetables that Mr. Menders and Mr. Scatt disregard due to their dainty appetites. Usually, there are several morsels remaining on their plates when the gentlemen repair from table. My brother scavenges these, and I must admit I enjoy watching him bat them around the room. (It is possible my brother is a "cat." I still can't remember his name, however... Mr. Scatt, may I depend on you?) He often leaves these pieces scattered to their corners when bored with his play, but as mentioned he does maintain a fondness for broccoli and truly gnaws those florets to powder.

This house is *full* of marvels, and I will commit myself to enumerating them in these pages. I am bursting to write them all down right now! Alas, I can't remember any at the moment... I enjoy so much my wanderings about, and yet it is difficult to *remember* most of my discoveries. Now that I possess this miraculous diary, I will finally be able to record my "adventures," such as they are, and in reading back, relive them—or, if I am a ghost, "rehaunt" them.

I am growing so tired, I'm afraid, feeling that dusky-dust weakness I'm prone to, and I will have to delay any further composition until tomorrow. I am still very excited, though, to begin this diary! Thank you so much, Fireman's Hat!

Second Day

Afternoon... Mr. Menders came at me with an axe this morning, hence my tardiness in attending to this diary. He encountered me in the pantry where I was tabulating the different varieties of Dry Goods, and as he happened to have the axe in his hand, he raised it and swung it with an agility that his lugubrious bones have rarely expressed. At least, I have not often witnessed such nimbleness on his part.

I scurried to safety under a shelf in the back behind the flour barrel and was terrified for a while as Mr. Menders continued to swing his axe at me and with his free hand reach about grasping with his rooky-hook fingers while foamy rivulets cataracted from his teeth and his crimson eyes glowed up like the winter sunset on twin lakes.

That is a *very* effective description, is it not? I am *very* proud of it. I hope if Mr. Scatt chances upon this diary, he will be *very* impressed with me. And I hope he will remonstrate Mr. Menders for his rudeness. I don't know what I ever did to Mr. Menders to inspire this grudge, or what aspect in my nature it may be that offends him so ceaselessly, but I am weary of escaping from his violence.

Fortunately, it is rare that Mr. Menders catches me off guard. I think I was a bit distracted this morning by all the excitement... my own *diary*! The object keeps rushing to my mind (which, unlike Mr. Menders, I maintain between my lungs, nestled cozily beneath my heart). Thus, I neglected to keep alert to the *sniff-sniff-sniff* that always precedes his entrances.

Later... I meant to mention earlier that there are so many *beans* in the pantry, I can hardly keep track of them all, yet the number of *lentils* is tiny indeed. I wonder what leads to such differences. And how are they replenished?... for they *do* reduce, those piles, oh yes, but they also increase. (Meanwhile, the precious sardine tins stand in a solemn stack, untouched for ages. If only my brother knew.)

Evening... What a lovely time I've had! My brother mostly pays no attention to me, whatsoever, but tonight, he snuggled! It is possible he sensed my desolation, as I was still feeling very put out by my morning's altercation with Mr. Menders. I was kneeling at the altar in the attic (hoping for some spiritual succor, which it's said the object will provide, although I've yet to receive it, on which account I certainly won't stop supplicating as there are ancillary benefits), when suddenly, I felt my brother's curling caresses in the small of my back, and I kept quite still while he pressed himself against me in delightful ways. Finally, he took himself into my lap and allowed me to hug him to my belly for a span of time, which I cherished most devoutly! I love my brother, diary, I really do, even though his words are sometimes cruel.

Third Day

Morning... I wish I could record a dream, since it's morning, but I never seem to remember my dreams. As a matter of fact, I don't even remember going to sleep, nor do I remember waking up. I remember writing in this diary, however—just last night! And here I am, once again, expending such massive effort to draw these words upon this book, one by one. But as for the intervening span, I simply cannot account for it.

You must understand my frustration. I love my brother, and I love Mr. Scatt, and I even tolerate Mr. Menders, but this *absence* that persists in afflicting my memory makes it so difficult for me to formulate a history of my own existence. For instance, I can't remember my mother, nor my father. It is to be supposed—is it not?—that I, being a girl, and my brother, being... my brother... cannot have appeared in the world spontaneously, but must have been *given rise to* by some set of *parents*. Mr. Scatt and Mr. Menders are both far too old to be my parents, and after all, that particular provenance is quite impossible for some other reasons that are not coming to mind. There are no other people in this house. Indeed, I have never seen any other person than those listed above.

I think I shall go weep somewhere. My tears will wet the couch cushions, and Mr. Menders will become enraged if he sits there... but I need to do it. I need to wail, also. It is called "keening," sometimes, as in "Mr. Scatt, her incendiary and intolerable *keening* destroys my mentation once again." Yes, "keening," I like that word very much.

[*Marginalis*] My dear, you are *Gracie*, and it is *Bob* who adores the broccoli. Do forgive *Mr. Menders*—his is a delicate constitution and a volatile temperament, but he truly is a lovely man in most respects, and of course, brilliant. (And I feel I should clarify, you were not born here, and indeed how you came here is a mystery to me; although I know nothing of your "parents," so perhaps I am mistaken. You are a most enchanting girl, however, and always welcome in our home.)

Yrs., *Scatt*.

p.s.—I am most *taken* by your descriptions, dear! That is to say, *impressed*. I hope you carry on with this project. I think it is a healthy occupation for you.

Evening... I am grateful that Mr. Scatt has chanced upon my diary and elucidated some details that had escaped me. My name is Gracie, I must strive to keep that word to hand at all times! Is it possible, I wonder, to craft a chalice of some kind, into which the name might be poured, and whenever I needed to remember it, I could simply drink from the chalice to revive the word to my mind? Because it is already escaping me, and I must move my gaze to Mr. Scatt's notation to retrieve it. Gracie. On its own line:

GRACIE. — G R A C I E —

This house is full of marvels, it occurs to me... and I wouldn't be the least surprised if I should find a *chalice* among its many treasures! My brother's name is Bob.

Bob Bob Bob.

BOB.

I shall begin my search right away, and I won't return to this diary until I have a chalice in my hand!

Fourth Day

Morning... As it happens, I have not yet found a chalice. In fact, I entirely forgot to search for it! Somehow, I got to counting beans again. I don't know why I must tabulate the Dry Goods, but I must. I confess, although I had been reluctant to admit it, hoping perhaps that the activity of composing sentences in my diary might take the place of that other loathsome compulsion... I devote more than half of my waking spans to my performance in the pantry, which is to say, *counting beans*, but I cannot remember how many beans there are, nor even lentils, nor even blasted sardine tins, although I can *see* them all clearly in my mind right now, and if I possessed a finger in my mind, I would count them to the last one and write the number in my diary and be done with it once and for all! Not true, however, for the piles are always expanding and shrinking, aren't they, the number is not fixed, I'll never know the answer, a fruitless enterprise, and yet I am utterly *obsessed* to count them, endlessly.

In any case, I believe it has been well more than a day since my prior entry in this diary, and it is possible it has been more than a week... has it been more than a year? I don't know. But it is certainly the Fourth Day, as far as diary entries go, so I will not attempt to alter my diary's calendar to accommodate vagaries of time, in which I have no discretion.

I have read back through my entries, and I am intrigued by the metaphor of the lakes, which I employed in rendering Mr. Menders' demonic eyes during his most recent attack. Let me set it down again, so I may contemplate it in tranquility: "His crimson eyes glowed up like the winter sunset on twin lakes." I don't think I have ever seen a lake, much less twin lakes, and what is the difference, pray, between a winter sunset and a summer one? I have seen the sun through certain windows, at times, but never in its state of "setting," regardless of season. I am at a loss as to how I developed that metaphor without having experience of any of the images it comprises.

Bob. Gracie. Those are delicious words, aren't they? I *must* find a chalice, so that I may drink them over and over again.

Fifth Day

Morning... I am so very excited, but confused! I have found a chalice, anyway, that's not confusing. But I have also found a little girl's dress beneath the beans! It fits me perfectly, I should say, and I am wearing it now. In it, I feel *myself*, somehow, as if before I had been missing some critical member of my anatomy—an arm or a head, for example—and now I've resecured it, whatever it was.

I may thank Bob for the discovery. (And I may thank this *chalice* for my swift recollection of my brother's lovely name!) I had found myself in the pantry, of course, counting everything up, and *Bob* joined me there, for a change. Usually, I must conduct my activities in the pantry all by myself. In fact, I don't believe my brother had ever been in the pantry before this morning—at least, not in *my* presence, which is a thing that occupies the pantry a good deal of the time, let me tell you! Indeed, if I could relocate my "presence" from its overly persistent haunt in the pantry to more congenial locales, I surely would, and you know it, diary.

As I was relating, Bob joined me, and I must add that I was woeful at the time—in fact, I was keening. I believe Bob would like to console his sister, occasionally, even if at other times he's cruel, and he did butt my shins a few times with his head as an *overture*, of sorts, to an *invitation* to affectionate snuggling, but he became distracted by the beans. Indeed, Bob became *very* interested, all of a sudden, in those beans! They are, it must be admitted, exceedingly conducive to productive scampering. A single swipe sends one winging to far-flung reaches of a room, and the only possible pursuit involves much leaping and prancing and posing, stimulations that my dear brother values to a high degree.

It so happened that on the *first* attempt, he lost his bean behind the flour barrel, and on his *second* attempt, the bean did skip up gaily onto a high shelf behind a row of pickling jars... and on the *third* attempt, and the *fourth*, and *etcetera* and so on!... Ha ha ha! Suffice it to say, after a succession of these thwarted bean-captures, Bob adopted an attitude of pent frustration, which—after a few preparatory, side-to-side shakings-out of the hindquarters—he unleashed most ferociously upon the main bean-pile by leaping frenziedly atop it, his body stretched out flat with all limbs askew (a most adorable position, I must insert!), and of course, the beans responded to this surge by immediately avalanching all over that little room! Bob continued to roll about ecstatically among the beans, somehow managing to assert his dignity even in such undignified array... and that's when I noticed that he was indeed *arrayed*, and not merely in beans,—but in the most delightful blue dress I had ever seen! (It must be acknowledged that it was the only blue dress I had ever seen.) The dissolution of the pile had uncovered the garb to view, and Bob's rolling among the beans had wrapped it around his head and forelegs to the degree that he was securely bound, so that he was struggling to remove himself. I tendered my assistance, and discovering that the beautiful little dress fitted my own body as if tailored especially for it, I of course donned the garment and even now I cannot prevent myself from caressing the fabric repeatedly (as if I would wish to prevent myself!).

The happy outcome of all this: I may confidently conjecture that I've been cured of my bean-counting! Time will tell, of course, but there is something different in me now that I am wearing this lovely dress... It is possible my attachment to the beans is much reduced, if not entirely severed. And I am feeling such a sensation of relief!

All the same, this effort of writing word after word upon the paper exhausts my energies, and I am currently too depleted to continue on to this narrative's outlandish, and even more sensational, sequel—The Adventure of the Chalice. I will pick up again later, if it's all the same to you (perhaps what I cherish most about you, my beloved diary—that it truly *is* all the same to you!).

And did I neglect to mention?... Attend, but first, allow me regally to quaff from yonder chalice!... *Ahem*. My name is Gracie! And may I introduce my brother Bob? Ah, my very own *chalice*... I can't wait to relate the details of its acquisition!

[*Marginalis*] I, too, await eagerly this interesting tale! —*Scatt*.

Evening... After much needed rest and recuperation, I am now prepared to describe The Adventure of the Chalice.

Having gained the little blue dress for myself, I found myself in exuberant spirits, and Bob behaving in a companionable manner, weaving among my steps and in general hewing near to me as I moved about the house, I decided the timing was auspicious for me to investigate a particular room, which in all other cases I have endeavored to avoid. For in my mind, just beneath my heart, an idea had been incubated some time earlier that possibly my best chance at finding the desired object of my searches would be had in the bedchambers of Mr. Menders. If anyone would keep a *chalice* among his belongings, it would be that man, whose *tastes* are so refined and exquisite, it may be agreed by all, even if his *passions* may become rather, at times, excessive. This being my diary, I sustain no fear of your disbelief, so I shall merely recount, without exaggeration, what happened upon mine and Bob's entrance into that mysterious bedroom, as fantastical as the subsequent events may seem:

As soon as my feet touched beyond the threshold, I found myself, along with my brother, in a vasty wintry field, its snowy expanses so blindingly white that they were actually a kind of *blue*. Strangely, my brother had taken on the form of a *boy*, still recognizably my brother by means of his scampering and playful demeanor, and yet lacking whiskers and paws, and also notably bulkier in mass. In the distance, I spied a spindly tree towering over a traveller's trunk. I traipsed as best I could across the crispy snow, and found it strange indeed that I left no footprints behind me, whilst my brother, in the shape of a boy, trailed behind him the footprints of a cat!

On reaching the trunk, I saw that the lid was securely shut, and I despaired of opening it, except that my brother, without the least hesitation, made a running leap upon the top, and the weight of his landing operated some mechanism that enabled the lid to spring open with force—enough force that my brother was sent splaying at the foot of the tree. As he recovered himself, and I saw that he was uninjured, I directed my attention to the contents of the trunk, which, to my initial disappointment, appeared simply to consist in a scattering of white bones. I would have turned away, but that I noticed, nearly hidden beneath their helter-skelter mound... what do you think? *A chalice*!

Of course, I picked it up, and as soon as I did so, a movement occurred in the vicinity of the tree that overhung this scene. I glanced there and saw that the tree was no tree after all, but *Mr. Menders*! (Had I been more alert, I would have noticed the characteristic *sniff-sniff-sniff* that had begun to intrude upon my hearing some moments earlier.) He stood with his arms both raised above him, in one hand an axe, on his head a Fireman's Hat, and behind him I saw two frozen lakes, the sun sinking into them and setting the ice ablaze, red flames stretching long, jagged fingers into the blackening firmament. As a matter of fact, I noticed that *all* was blackened, even including the field of snow,—which, now that I was paying close attention, no longer was snow at all, but rather, *velvet* like the soft lining of the trunk in which I'd discovered my chalice and over which I still was bent, the poll of Mr. Menders' axe nuzzling the back of my neck to provide an endpoint of the arc his swing would describe once he'd succeeded in lifting the weapon and flipping the blade into a severing angle.

I did scream, I admit, and perhaps it was this lapse of *my* courage that inspired my *brother's* courage, for he leapt upon me and spilled me across the floor just as the blade swooped down—through that very space lately occupied by my head!—and smashed instead into the pile of bones within the trunk, and I am thankful that I retained enough sensibility to clutch my newfound *chalice* close to my chest as I rolled away and found myself not in any field, nor in any trunk, but in the hallway outside of Mr. Menders' bedchambers. Bob was with me, returned to his proper shape and form, and he was even scraping away the tears from my cheeks with his pointy-peck tongue, which brought me to my senses by means of a giggling spate that seized me even as I fled away toward the attic, fearful (within my mirth) of pursuit even though there was no sign of Mr. Menders.

This chalice is an *objet d'art*, truly, and so uniquely crafted! There is no stem nor base, but the bowl is broad at bottom so that it could be set upon a table without fear of tipping out its contents, and yet there are three *finger-holes* on one side for ease of carrying. Indeed, that is how I carried it as I sought out my diary, most eager to submit my newfound treasure to its fine utility. And so I took up these pages and from them read my name into the chalice, as well as my brother's name, and indeed every word that I have written here, so that all is stored safely in that cup as a tasty wine of memory that I may drink whenever I wish to remember something that might have happened.

The room grows dark... and I feel heavy and exhausted from this writing, but all the same, I have just got an idea that I might pursue tomorrow!... for is it not possible, it occurs to me, that my mind beneath my heart resides in merely *temporary* housing?... inadequate to hold a voluminous reservoir of memory, such as I require... and perhaps a more *permanent* and *suitable* shelter may be had within this strangely shaped, but copious, *chalice* I have found?

[*Marginalis*] Both *Mr. Menders* and myself have discovered a sorrowful loss this morning. I shall leave this note along the edges here in order to keep these pages blank... in the probably vain hope that someday a particular little girl will *return* from wherever she has been *spirited away to*... and write more enchanting words upon the paper of this book. This "chalice" (so delightful!) along with your diary, dear child, shall be safely ensconced inside the helmet, should you ever need them.

Yrs., *Scatt.*

p.s.—I promise, your heroic *Bob* will be cared for as he always has been; indeed, he will *feast* on those sardines!

FEVER VISIONS

"If you are lucky," her mother told Hattie, "Visions will accompany your fever. They arrive from Hell, for the most part, but they are usually harmless... if a bit *warm*."

Her smile was reassuring and kind, and she patted her daughter's forehead with a damp rag.

"Just stay cool," she advised. "Enjoy the show, but watch you don't get drawn in, or you'll become a vision yourself! There's a notebook and pencil on your night-table, dear— keep track of those visions... I think they'll prove most enlightening when the fever's broken, and I look forward to reading your account."

Mother's blue, wise eyes sparkled with mirth, and she floated out of the room amidst copious skirts, dabbing the rag to her own perspirations as she eased the door shut behind her.

Hattie waited patiently, but no visions were forthcoming... only that unrelenting sensation from her ribs of an iron grip upon them... the ceaseless, wrenching claws of her disease that had seized (and not stopped rattling) her bones from the fever's inception... a monstrous creature roaming her guts and shredding them gleefully. It was called V'Eye Rust, and she believed it was named after its lone, corroded eye, a grim and glowing apparatus with the lids flecked away by their exposure to her organismic fluids, leaving that malignant stare perpetually unshrouded...

That was no vision, however, but conventional allegory; indeed, a most unexceptional and tiresome one. Sheer make-believe... What was the use? It was *all* so wearying, being sick. And tedious! When exactly were these *visions*—the proper ones—scheduled to show up? At least Hell would be an entertainment, a diversion from her current misery... if it would simply *appear*, as had been promised!

Finally, to the blessed relief of one very sick little girl, Hattie's fevered visions commenced (as did her journal of them).

How shall I tell it, Mother? As if it is happening, or as if it has happened? I don't know which mode betrays the truth worse. I shall have to choose, I suppose... You knew I should have to, didn't you? (And didn't say anything—so, so tricksy, Mother!) All right, I will begin the vision...

The house is on fire. At least, I think it is. The awareness has struck me suddenly. Previously, I had been drowsing and slightly melancholic—as I often become in the stillness of midafternoon, even when I am well—but now I smell an acrid smoke, and heat weighs oppressively down on me from all sides. Out the window upon the treetops are heaving shadows of pumpkin orange and deep blue, swarming about with no rhythm, but unhurriedly.

Seemingly, it is nighttime, but how? The sunlight has fled away from the world... and all at once, not at the usual stately pace.

I slip out of bed and put on my dressing gown. Before the door, I hesitate, holding my hand near the knob. Detecting no radiation from it, I enclose it in my palm and gentle the door ajar. When I release the knob, the door swings away as if falling.

The hallway is pitch black, and I am greatly afraid to enter it, but I seem to be walking forward by no command of my own... as if some other girl inhabits this body, and I have been brought along as a guest, disallowed from interfering with events.

Is this the nature of a vision? All sight and no power?

And whose body is it? May I call it mine, anymore, even though it fails to heed me? I can assure you, Mother, I am wailing to turn back! The terror of the void is upon me!

For I am surging forward into a pitch black world that contains not even one sparkle of luminescence, a universe without ground and sky, in which nothing exists but my observation.

And yet, to my relief, I realize there is a color upon it. It is not a pitch black world, after all, more of a pitch orange, if that can be.

I am inside of an orb, it occurs to me, constructed of fire, explaining the heat. Indeed, I begin to perceive the flickering of that flame, its hazy edges contrasted to the dusky blue abyss behind.

Suddenly, from that abyss, a face inserts between the tongues of fire. To my surprise, I recognize it is my own face!

I look down at my body and note that I am in fact not myself, but a spider. I have eight legs, all scrambling to avoid the flames.

I activate my million limbly joints and rush upon that face, clicking my mandibles together madly as I seek to destroy the flesh and feed upon it. As I sink my pincers into the lovely feminine cheek, I perceive that this face is not my face at all; it is yours, Mother.

And yet, I am in my bed, aren't I? It was only a vision, wasn't it?

Delighted, but weakly, I take up my notebook and pencil... and what you've just read is the composition that has resulted. Reading back, I approve of it, but I would not dare to show it to my teacher!

She would certainly criticize the tense... I see now I made a mistake; I should have chosen past, not present.

I'll do better next time. For now, I feel unwell and must nap.

Hattie swam up from a deep cauldron of sleep to perceive her mother's face gazing down lovingly upon her from high up. A cool rag dampened her forehead here and there, pressed into contact by firm fingertips.

Her mother's eyes glowed a deep blue, casting beams that sought Hattie's own eyes.

The girl began to speak, but her mother shushed her, so she sank back into the Lethean water, but not before noticing those tiny, twinned scabs upon her mother's left cheek.

I awoke from my nap straight into a vision! (Note that I am now employing the past tense.)

The ground about me was soft and loamy. No bed, no dresser, no night-table was in evidence. My room had been spirited away, or else I had been spirited away from it.

I was inside a garden, I realized. I say "inside" because there was a roof upon it. A marble roof, as it featured majestic, geological swirls; but simultaneously, the roof was glass, for I could see through it to the unclouded, daytime sky.

A rainbow column reached from a fountain at the garden's center into the peak of the roof, as if holding it aloft. I wandered toward that column, fascinated by the colors, which were not the usual violets and yellows and oranges that one sees in a rainbow, but were pale and pinkish in varying hues. Spectral, you might call it. A ghost column, perhaps... I felt calm and free to speculate.

As I drew near to the fountain, a god emerged from the water, cataracts cascading off him as he rose to his full height, which was higher somehow than the garden's roof. He stood tall and naked, and I averted my eyes. His legs were massive snakes, his feet their heads, and from his toes a multitude of forked tongues hissed out at me.

I fell back screaming, but I could not flee as my legs had disappeared. My arms were also missing. I was only a torso and head, wallowing in the billows of my night-dress.

The god's baritone voice swooped in, reassuring me that there was no harm where he walked. He did not use language to communicate, however, for his voice was only a wind, a mighty breath before which were flattened the flowers of the garden, and I don't know how I understood him.

The sky gloomed, and the roof dissolved into a rocky rain upon us. The naked god blew a sweet breeze over me to send astray from harming me those descending minerals and crystals.

Don't be fretted, Mother, for I never allowed my eyes to perceive his nakedness. And when the breeze had blown over, so had the vision, and I found I was in my bed, feeling quite cool and collected.

I feel wondrous, in fact! Although, my sheets are sopping wet and quite uncomfortable; I look forward to your changing them.

Hattie decided to change her sheets herself, rather than wait for her mother to look in, but she had overestimated her condition. She fell in a heap to the floor and was too weak to haul herself back onto the mattress.

When her mother swept in sometime later, she was naturally horrified to find her daughter in disarray and set herself immediately to bustling about: bundling the daughter in a blanket and setting her on the chair by the desk—peeling the sheets from the mattress and replacing them with fresh ones from the hallway closet—and laying the daughter down to snuggle cozily into the new, warm nest she had made.

Hattie truly loved her mother (especially when she felt so vulnerable and cared for) and murmured something along those lines; her mother hissed pleasantly, tickling her earlobe with a quick, forked tongue before hurrying off to the sound of a buzzer in a faraway room. Hattie thought it was the dryer, but there were so many appliances, who could keep track?

I hardly know how I'll set this down. I'm feeling rather light-headed, and it's even difficult to breathe, much less direct a pencil across these lines. I've committed myself, however, to this project, and I'm determined I will not flag in my effort, especially as this particular vision seems to me the most critical one I've experienced.

Somehow, I was in the attic, and I knew right away it was a vision, since I didn't remember getting myself there. And besides, how could I have pulled down the stairs by myself? Impossible, really. As a matter of fact, I don't think I've ever been in the attic before... maybe once when I was quite little.

After some amount of time, in which I'm not sure how I occupied myself, I realized that the room was very messy, and I decided to clean it up. (I'll admit, it also occurred to me that my father would be so pleased with my industry!) Soon, I was sweeping furiously with a straw broom and moving items around from spot to spot. I don't know how effective my cleaning was.

Then I noticed that the window looked out on dirt, just dirt—as if the whole house, right to the tippy-top, had been buried... possibly in a Himalayan avalanche!

I ran to the window and tried to raise it, but it was stuck. Which was for the best, I think: what if I'd succeeded, and all that dirt came flowing in? On the other hand, it hardly matters, does it, since it was only a vision.

I started to hear sounds from below. Quite frightening sounds... moans of anguish possibly. And glee. Someone was gleeful, and he may have been muttering something, but I couldn't make out what he said. It was definitely a he, at least.

It being a vision, I moved to locate the source of the sounds, even while I begged myself desperately not to investigate.

I traveled down the stairs. There were a great many stairs... more stairs, I think, than our house actually contains. I descended flight after flight of them. For hours, it seemed, I did nothing but approach those low sounds, which always seemed to be floating up from some incredible depth.

Then, suddenly, I was in a blue room, and the sounds were very loud, although I still couldn't make out what was being said... if anything at all was being said. Perhaps it wasn't a room, though, for there were no furnishings, and its shape was spherical. There was a round window nearby, and I peered out of it.

Through the window, I saw a vast chamber extending so far that I could not see any walls. More concentrated inspection revealed that a dark, viscid river flowed across the granite floor. I did not want to know what that fluid was... since I was fairly certain I knew what it was.

At that moment, I became a sort of cyclone, gusting out the window and blowing around the chamber at an exhilarating speed, round and round. During these cycles, I saw a great many human bodies that were misformed and bent into hideous—in retrospect, quite piteous—shapes, and they were operating strange, ancient-looking machines whose possible uses I could not deduce. Items emerged from toothy, metallic orifices and were transported on production belts, and I thought perhaps this was a factory of some kind.

And then I stopped whirling and became a little girl again. But I could not have been myself because I saw myself standing in the corner... I'm not certain I can write this, but I am resolved, I must: my legs were spread, and I perceived between them the source of that ichorous river I'd witnessed earlier...

Then, to my horror (but I confess, with shame, also to my relief), I saw that the girl in the corner wasn't me, after all... it was you, Mother! Your face was an agony, and the river flowed more and more copiously from between your legs until the chamber was filled and everyone and everything in it floating hopelessly about.

Among the rapids that developed, there were babies. I saved one, reached out and grabbed it and held it to my chest, but there were so many others, all crying and wailing, all lost to the torrent and doomed, and I couldn't hope to save them too, so I just held on to the one I had.

I admit, even though it was only a vision, and I knew it, I still wept and wept as I was carried along. Wept for all those babies and wept for you, Mother, for it seemed to me your pain was infinite.

And then the river emptied into a lake, and I splashed about, clutching to the baby I'd saved, which slept peacefully and made no movement nor any sound. For that, I was grateful indeed!

I am almost to the end of this vision now... but I've reached the most dreadful part. For around me floated the corpses of all the babies I had not rescued. All of them were dead. But thankfully, it was only a vision.

A smiling mouth with rusted teeth, situated upon the end of a long and narrow proboscis, emerged from below the surface of the lake and began moving among the babies, slurping them up like sodden Cheerios. They made bulges in the tube that progressed its length as they were swallowed down.

I screamed at this mouth to stop, but it only snapped its teeth together and gnashed them gratingly, producing a sickening squeal of metal against metal. Having noticed me, the monster to whom this mouth belonged rose bodily from the lake... and I saw its corroded eye, its baleful stare... and it began to move toward me... toward me and my little baby.

For I knew now that it was my own little baby that I held, the baby I would someday bring into the world when I myself became a mother!

Therefore, before the monster reached me, I grew my fingernails very long and with them scooped out my own eye. Into it, I placed my beautiful, sleeping baby and set it sailing on the waves.

And then I was sucked into that awful mouth...

Hattie was on fire. Her clothes were ashes around her, and she knew that soon the bed would go up too, so she ran to the window and leapt out, hoping to be doused by some rain, if it chanced to be raining. It didn't occur to her that being on the second floor, she was bound to fall a great distance... Fortunately, her mother was waiting for her and caught her; indeed, her mother grew into a great tree in the yard whose branches held the little girl protectively aloft without themselves catching fire. All night, the sky glowed crimson in reflection of Hattie's flames, and she shivered violently and continuously in her mother's leafy cradle, hardly aware of anything that was happening.

By morning, the fever had broken, and Hattie's mother brought her into the house, dressed her in clean pajamas, and tucked her back into bed to enjoy a restful slumber.

When Hattie awoke, breathing easily and enjoying the window's exuberant transmission of the sun's beams onto her bedspread, she noticed a bell on her night-table and rang it vigorously. Within moments, the door swung open and her father rushed across the threshold. His worried eyes relaxed and smiled when he saw her sitting up and healthy, and he fell to his knees at the bedside, hugging his daughter to his cheek.

"You're finally well!" he said.

"I'm finally *hungry*," Hattie replied, and they both laughed.

"Of course, dear, I'll bet you're famished! How does a huge breakfast of bacon and eggs and buttered toast sound?"

"Delicious!" Hattie giggled. "Oh, and my mother, please call my *mother*... all those feverish *visions* I had... The journal was a brilliant idea! If it weren't for that, I swear I'd have been *lost*, utterly lost..."

Her father looked helplessly and wordlessly upon her until Hattie remembered that her mother had been dead for many years; she had never known her.

"I'm sorry," she said. "The fever... I forgot myself."

Her father put his arm around her shoulders. "Nothing to apologize for, Hattie, nothing."

After an awkward moment, her voice trembling, Hattie said, "It was me, wasn't it? I never put it together before. She died because of me..."

"No!" Her father pulled back and peered intently into her eyes. "Don't ever think that. It wasn't you. She caught a sickness, that's all. It was afterward. There was no connection."

"A fever?"

"Yes. Very high."

"She was delirious?"

"Yes. It was all too much in the end. Too much and too much. But you lived, Hattie, you lived, and for that we're all so grateful!"

And it was off to breakfast then, and she soon found herself roundly crushing her older brother at chess while her father made jests at the boy's expense. Fortunately, her brother was a good sport about it, considering her recent illness.

NANCY & HER MAN

With so many graves to choose from, Herman wondered, how did the girl with fairy wings happen to alight on *his*? The cemetery was full. There were many thousands of headstones, and nothing distinguished his plot in particular from the others… no stirring epitaphs, no effusive sprays of wildflowers.

The girl danced with a skillful abandon upon his headstone, a talented unknowing. Her tiny wings flapped adorably when she remembered to pull a string; they also fluttered to greet the languid breeze that sauntered through the rows. Little bells sewn into the fringes happily chorused their devotions to that airy passage.

Herman had, until this moment, presumed himself dead, since he slept eternally in a coffin, never waking nor even turning his cheek to seek a cooler portion of the pillow (all portions being equally cool, truth be told, but let us not confuse our hero), yet here he was enjoying this fairy girl's decidedly impromptu and uninvited (but entirely delightful) performance over his gravesite. A sign of life! Or, at least: a posthole for a sign, pending delivery.

He thought of our dancer as a girl, but face it, she was in her thirties. Perhaps it was the fairy wings that lent her the girlish aspect, perhaps her slight frame or her whimsical bob. Detailed inspection reveals from her flesh, however, the harrowed textures of experience. As much as I would like to caress a fair, unblemished maiden's cheek, I can not tell a lie.

The girl—deferring to Herman's nomination—is not below thirty-five, but also not possibly older than forty. Her wings, as averred by a receipt itemizing raw materials from a local crafts store, are less than an hour old. The receipt is stowed within a stylish New Yorker tote crumpled nearby in the grass, which I am quite persuaded belongs to her.

I wonder if she knows that her tap-dancing has awakened the dead!

At least: one of the dead.

Hmm.

On further consideration, it *would* seem foolish to assign to the category of dead things a man who clearly is not dead... Herman observes, approves, even applauds dear Becky's rhythmic effusions upon his grave. Shall I amend my statement? Yes: her tap-dancing has, even temporarily, diverted Herman from his delusion of death. A recommendation, I dare say, for the power of Art to effect positive change in the lives of real people. A public service message.

Yes, Becky. A perfectly fine name, don't you think? It may or may not be hers in actuality, but lacking evidence, I can, for now, do no better. She paid cash for the craft items—thus, no name on the receipt—and she carries no identifying documents. In all likelihood, she lives nearby and walked straight here.

Dissatisfied with his angle on the scene (and with some difficulty due to intervening matter), Herman extricated himself from his coffin and brushed the wrinkles from his jacket. The drabness of his suit embarrassed him under the circumstances: the world around him was all colors and cheer! A yellow sun nuzzled a blue sky, and a chipper avian chorus serenaded our fluid, limber fairy dancer. The setting called for blithe spirits and light fabrics, not stiff shoulders and rough, gray wool. He was overdressed to say the least, but surely worse would have been his nudity. It is important to maintain one's sense of perspective.

Becky nodded minutely (but politely) in acknowledgement when she noticed Herman watching her, and kept right on dancing, her mien pleased and lightened by his attention's updraft. Herman, determined to loosen up, reclined on both elbows in the grass and contented his gaze with her sinuous movements. It felt like years since he had been given the opportunity to appreciate such gorgeous limbs describing graceful lines; indeed, it *had* been years. By the dates carved into the headstone, we may venture, more than ten.

A performance has a natural lifespan, much as an organism does. It begins in mystery, propagates allure with all its prowess, achieves an energetic crescendo, then comprehends its final purpose and dissipates into its surroundings. Soon, the elements are reassembled and the process recapitulated. Given patience, we (the audience) shall never need to leave our seats: the show must go on!

Lightly fatigued, Becky lowered herself by an invisible cinch and perched with fairy litheness on the grass. She dug her fingers into the soil between the blades and brought up some cool crumbles of the ancient earth.

"Would you like some?"

Herman realized suddenly that he was famished and did not hesitate to accept the proffered nourishment. Together they munched on the dirt, and Herman found his tongue pleasantly loosened, to the degree at least that he said, "Thank you, dearie," which prompted Becky's giggling rebuke, "I'm Nancy, not Dearie!" Nor, it seems, Becky. I stand corrected.

A beam, invisible but felt, protruded from the notch between his eyebrows and bumped against her cheek. "A pleasure, Nancy dear, I'm certain. It seems so long since I uttered a sentence... even a word... When was the last time?"

Nancy shrugged and brushed some silty crumbs from her dress. She tucked her chin bashfully into her clavicle and did not dare to meet his cool gaze. "You only have today to make more of them. As many words as you like, but only today. Would you like to spend it with me?"

He looked around at the grass, the stones, the Gothic decor, so staid and traditional yet never out of style for those of a certain temperament. A pleasant enough setting, if not particularly stimulating. Nancy caught the color of his appraisal and quickly interjected, "We won't stay here, of course. There's lots to do in town. It's not far."

Herman nodded solemnly and turned his regard back toward this singular fairy princess, whose face and bodily structure one really felt compelled to keep studying. "That sounds a delight, Nancy. Will there be a lot of walking, though? I have to say, I feel a bit stiff for that."

Nancy giggled, "I'll assist you, if need be... but I think you'll loosen up soon enough. You'd be amazed what a little movement can do for tight muscles!"

"You are a marvelous dancer, if you don't mind my saying so. Speaking of movement."

Nancy glowed under the beam of his approval. "Thank you so much, darling!" More diffidently, "I was practicing for weeks."

"Time well spent, then. Hmm. I have to confess, Nancy, it occurs to me now... I'm not entirely sure how I've been spending my time lately. Not practicing, certainly. In fact, I wonder what I would practice?"

"The first thing to practice is breathing. Trust me, once

you have the basics down, the rest comes *so* easy."

"Ah! A thing to start with, then… breathing. Like this?" He braced himself to take a deep breath, but rolled over on his side instead. Nancy rolled with him (carefully—preserving her wings) to save him from embarrassment. He nodded gratefully and tried again with a hair less force. A whistle sounded from his throat; a bird on the headstone two rows down offered a conversational reply.

They worked on Herman's breathing for several minutes, and in short order, his respirations were as vigorous as one could hope for after such a prolonged lapse. At any rate, Nancy warmly praised his progress—Herman welcomed *any* source of warmth with pleasure.

"Now for walking," said Nancy. "The first step is to stand up."

"That's a large step."

Nancy supplied some lift, but Herman was pleased to find his own muscular reserves mostly adequate to the task. The snack had done wonders for his energy! However, he had to admit, a certain lethargy lingered in his eyeballs… and sluggishness entwined his limbs.

Nancy brushed some particles from the shoulder of his jacket, smoothed his lapels, and straightened his tie. "You know what would really hit the spot?" she asked.

"A comet?"

She giggled. "No! Well, I don't know, I guess it would, wouldn't it? Silly boy! I was thinking coffee?"

"That would also hit the spot," agreed Herman.

Nancy cupped his elbow and guided him onto the cemetery road. They proceeded toward the gate at a processional pace. Nancy's bells issued a cheerful counting of the steps, and

Herman nodded politely to every jingle until Nancy whispered in his ear to stop. He nodded politely to her and halted.

"No," she said, "By 'Stop' I meant 'Stop nodding at my bells.' We should continue walking!"

"Yes, that sounds pleasant," nodded Herman, stumbling into motion right away.

Nancy took his hand in hers and guided him through the gate. The café was not far away—two, maybe three blocks—but at their stately speed, they spent a good half-hour in transit. Nancy monitored his breathing and encouraged his progress with periodic compliments—to which, without fail, he replied, "Thank you, Nancy."

A black, wireframe table on the café's outdoor patio attracted Herman's fascination, and he made hopeful motions in its direction. Nancy indulged his enthusiasm and assisted him into the miniature wireframe chair that accompanied it. He rested his forearm on the mesh tabletop and with his fingers beat a metronomic tattoo. Nancy wandered inside to place their order at the counter.

From his patio'd perch, Herman drank in the stream of street life… appreciated the variety of people, animals, and machines all cavorting together and sharing the precious world amongst themselves so casually and carelessly. It had been quite some time since he'd partaken of such sights and sounds. Indeed… any sights and sounds. More accustomed to eternal darkness and morbid silence in an atmosphere of decrepitude and moral apathy, he found the fresh air and open acoustics quite stimulating if he did say so himself!

Nancy returned bearing twin ceramic coffee bowls and placed Herman's before him. He reached out but found his attempt to lift it stymied by a deficit of fingers.

"I seem to be having some trouble with my coffee," he said.

Nancy, who had been engaged in gentle blows and sips, peeked over at his situation, sighed a little sorrowfully, and pointed to the tabletop, where his fingers were wedged into the diamonds of the mesh. "Already?" she asked.

"At least I still have this." He presented a thumbs-up sign.

Nancy pouted. "Oh dear, it all blows by so quickly, doesn't it?"

"Yes, it is a lovely breeze, Nancy."

She had been preparing to essay a more expressive sort of wallowing sigh, but it evaporated into a giggle. "You." She put three affectionate pats on his shoulder, then—one by one, with pains to avoid damage—retrieved the fingers from the mesh and dropped them into her tote.

Herman leaned in to sniff his coffee, which continued to emanate copious steam, almost audible in its enthusiasm. And such an aroma! Pungent enough to wake the dead! Two magic ropes rose from the bowl, probed tentatively at his nostrils, and from there surged boldly into all the channels of his head. He hooked his thumb through the wide handle and cradled the bowl with his other hand, lifting it cautiously to his lips for an exploratory sip. Chocolate flavored dirt.

"Delicious!" he said. "What a day for sensations!"

"Yes," Nancy returned, "I'm so happy to share it with you, darling. Do you remember your last cuppa?" She dipped her face level with her own bowl on the tabletop and performed some raucous slurps.

He pondered. The past was a mist enshrouding myste-rious pulsations of light and sound. Those pulsations were significant, but he did not know of what. Thus, he sadly did not remember any other cuppas... but he was grateful for the current cuppa.

"Thank you for the current cuppa, Miss," he said.

At that moment, his thumb fell off. The bowl he had been holding tumbled to the tabletop, landing sideways then rolling upright with a grunt; a notable share of coffee slopped down through the mesh to splash his pants below.

"Oh, darling!" Nancy ran into the café and reemerged with a sizable stack of napkins in hand. She knelt before him and applied them firmly around his soggy thighs. "Are you hurt?" she asked.

"Not at all, dearie. Nancy."

"Do you feel it?"

"Admirable pressure. You clearly know what you are do-ing."

"No, silly, I mean the hot coffee! You're not scalded?"

"Hmm. You're right! I suppose I do feel something hot down there... a sensation of some kind... through many layers of something or other... a not-pleasant sensation." Suddenly, a beetle (teardrop-shaped) climbed out from behind his eyelid, paused to take its bearings, then slalomed recklessly down his cheek for a scurrying plunge behind his necktie knot.

"Oh boy, I didn't mean to... I'm just making things worse! Oh, never mind. Don't think about it, darling."

"Thank you, Nancy, I won't. Something of a relief."

Nancy plucked the perished thumb from the table and patted it dry with a napkin, then stowed it in her tote with the other fingers.

"We're gathering quite a collection already," she mur-mured.

"I wonder if you're feeling all right, Miss?" asked Herman

with some concern.

"Call me Nancy, won't you? And yes, I'm feeling marvelous, if you must know!" She summoned a puckish smile and (gently!) batted his bicep with her knuckles.

"I am happy to hear that! I must say, I have had a good feeling about you all along, Nancy. Thank you for taking me out. So refreshing after such a long... something."

"Such a long nap?"

"Was that what it was? I thought it was a death, but I am ready to admit to any misapprehension on my part... indeed, hopeful to admit."

"I was being euphemistic, darling. Since you were unable to name it the first time."

Herman nodded to her. "Ah yes, I see... but not unable. I was searching for, but failed to find, a more... kindly word than death. Since you are still alive."

"For the moment, so are you."

He looked out across the patio at nothing in particular—or rather, perhaps, at everything—then back at Nancy. "So it seems!" With pleasure (and an involuntary squeak from his grimed, clogged lungs), he lifted the bowl to his lips and took a sip of the now lukewarm brew.

"Do you remember anything at all, darling?"

"Certainly. I remember watching you dance on my headstone. That was very lovely. I remember talking with you. I remember walking, and your bells tinkled in a way that drew my attention. The sun was above, and the birds were about. I remember many things!"

"Do you remember anything... from, you know... before all that?"

"No. Sadly, if there is anything else that happened to

me, Nancy, it is not in here." He pointed at his head, only to realize, with some disappointment, there were no fingers to point with. Then he brightened, recalling that the other hand remained digitally equipped, and switched to that one, lowering the first to his lap, out of sight beneath the tabletop. Nancy smiled warmly and reached across the table, leaning in and beckoning him to place the fingered hand between hers, for her to pet and fondle while they talked.

"Are you glad to be with me today?" she asked.

"I am delighted to make your acquaintance, dearie. Nancy! A pleasure, a pleasure."

"Are you curious about me, darling?"

"Yes! With all those gravestones to choose from, how did you happen to choose mine, I wonder? For your lovely dance, I mean."

She touched her chin to her shoulder and looked at him sideways. Insinuatingly, "Do you have any ideas?"

"No. Although, hmm. That way you just looked at me. Sideways. Do it again?" She performed as requested. "Yes, it is familiar to me! Do I know you, Nancy?"

"Maybe," she said. "Do you?"

"Ah. A subtle distinction. The better question being, then, do you know me, Nancy?"

"That is a much better question, James. And I'm happy to answer it with a big, fat 'Yes!' "

James looked out again across the patio, trying to see things through his new name... his eyebeam alighting on so many points in space and time that he could not tabulate them all... instead blurring them at once into a congeries of complex associations... pulsations of light and sound... mist-enshrouded.

He tested the word on his tongue: "James?" It didn't sound right… or perhaps it did. Nancy seemed very sincere, after all, in her assertion. Have I been lying to you, dear readership? In so fundamental a matter as a name? A literary scandal in the making… Let us hope there is an innocent explanation for all this!

"Didn't you notice it on your headstone?"

"Interestingly, I never thought to read my headstone. I was 100% enthralled by your performance."

She tucked her buoyant smile bashfully into her clavicle. "Oh, James, you're too much!"

"Is that why things keep falling off, I wonder?" He held up his arm, now lacking his hand, which was still being caressed by Nancy on the tabletop.

"Oh dear, there we go again," said a very wistful fairy girl, sliding the hand delicately into her tote.

To cheer her up: "May I hear the bells again, Nancy?"

Success! Her puckish smile hopped back upon her lips, and she gave her string three sharp tugs. Her wings rustled and the bells affirmed their pleasure at being included in the conversation.

James nodded to the bells and said to Nancy, "Lovely sounds. You are a lovely girl altogether. I am a very lucky corpse! I wonder why I thought my name was Herman."

Nancy burst into laughter (the bells joining in). "You thought you were Herman?"

"Yes, I was under that impression."

"Herman was your stage name, darling."

"Oh." He considered the information. "I was a stage?"

"No, a performer on a stage. You were Herman He-Man, Lord of the Yucks." I shall count this revelation as full exoneration for any and all previously construed narratorial hijincks. I am sorely disappointed in your lack of trust. Case closed. "You don't remember?"

Peering into the mist... "I'm afraid not."

Nancy's lower lip curled up and nuzzled her front teeth. "But you do remember a little bit, don't you... 'Herman' stuck, if nothing else."

"Who were these Yucks that I commanded?"

More merriness from Nancy, bells on backup. "They weren't people, they were laughs. You were a comedian."

"How interesting."

"Do you know what that is?"

"As a matter of fact, I am having some trouble bringing that definition to mind."

"It's a person who stands on a stage and says funny things to make an audience laugh."

"I see. So I commanded the audience, and the Yucks were my decrees."

"No, silly! Although... that's not entirely inaccurate. You have a way of putting things, don't you?"

"How did I die?"

"Oh. It was... an accident."

"In the line of duty?"

"No! Well, ha, sometimes. I won't deny, from time to time you may have died on stage, it happens to everyone, but you always came back. You killed way more than you died! You could make them love you no matter what. It was a special gift."

"I was a great warrior, then."

"Comedian."

"How many times did I die?"

"Oh... thousands, darling... over and over. It was the only thing you were good at! Should've seen yourself... Sisyphus and his boulder you were with the Yucks... night after sweaty night in a dead room... ha ha ha! The look on your face right now!"

"Is it funny? The look?"

"Yes, of course. You're a very funny man, even in your present condition. But don't get the wrong idea. You only died once, darling... in the way that matters."

"Perhaps a good thing, since my comedy was so poor."

"Oh now, I was just teasing you. You were very funny, and many people died of Yucks in the audiences under your command."

James nodded. "Thank you, Nancy, for filling in the blanks. It confirms my sense of my own greatness. I am glad I was such a ferocious comedian. Have very many history books been written about me yet?"

"You silly! Let's get off this topic, shall we? Even in death, you're all brags."

"Yes, we should explore other topics. For example, I am interested in Mr. Doggo. Could you tell me more about him?"

"Mr. Doggo?"

"The gentleman with his snout in your bag, I was wondering, is he an invited guest? He is certainly an impressive one."

Nancy, startled, now noticed the German Shepherd nuzzling in her tote. She scooted her chair back and smacked him smartly on his thick skull, but he calmly ignored her and continued to poke his nose into the Second Wonder of the Aromatic World... the First being a T-Bone steak—from the neighboring bistro, which shared the café's patio—still haunting his nostrils; his master had refused to share it with him only ten minutes earlier, severely wounding his fragile canine emotions and sending him into a tailspin of heart-rending trauma, from which he was able to recover only upon encountering the sensual summons of Nancy's tote.

She smacked the dog again, then placed both hands against his muscular neck and began shoving. "Shoo! Get out of there!" Desperation in her voice.

James leaned forward to assist, pressing his stump against the side of Mr. Doggo's face, who suddenly removed his toothy muzzle from the tote and snatched at James's forearm (Third Wonder)—surprised and delighted to discover it so loosely held by its owner—then hightailed it off the patio and disappeared around the corner.

"It seems my suit is no longer the perfect fit." Indeed, the sleeve dangled rather unattractively from his elbow, the new terminus of his arm. Nancy squeezed and tugged the limp cloth and began to weep. James said, "I don't feel any the worse for it, Nancy."

"You don't understand. I have to return you whole. Every piece of you. Otherwise, that's it."

"What's it?"

"The end! Of all this!"

James looked around at all this.

Nancy sighed. "You don't remember—you never do—but we do this every year. Our coffee. Our promenade. La-de-da. It's kind of a special day. But there are Rules, and one of them is that you have to go back exactly as you came."

"What will happen?"

"Nothing. We just won't be able to do this again. Today will be the last time."

"Ah. Then I suppose that makes this coffee all the more

precious, for being the last."

Nancy wiped her cheeks and sniffled. "That is one way of looking at it. Fucking dog."

"And that is yet another."

Nancy laughed in spite of herself. Not pleasantly, however. "Let's blow this joint," she said with a rough shake of her wings, provoking an insolent protest from the bells.

"Blow—?"

"Let's scram! Skedaddle! Vamoose!" Hectic in her cheeks. A flutter in her eyelid. A panting mouth.

"This is also familiar," said James.

Nancy turned away, held herself tense, squeezed her eyes shut, and then relaxed. "Is it?"

"Yes. I sense things in the mist…"

" 'The mist'?" She placed her palms over her ears. "Don't tell me! I don't want to know what's in there."

"Thank you, Nancy. I didn't want to look. It is a relief to refrain from knowing things."

She sank onto the perch of her flimsy wireframe chair and regarded her companion with grave affection. "Mmm. You're right, James, it really is."

"The coffee has perked me up, I find, Nancy. Maybe let's walk some more? I could use the exercise."

"Yes!" Springing to her feet, "Let's walk until the sun goes down, darling. If this is going to be the last time, then I want to treasure it all up!" Deliberately ignoring the lumpish tote on the table, Nancy hooked James's arm with her own and (carefully!) assisted him up. Together, they descended from the patio and commenced their promenade. We shall leave them to it…

Some hours later, post-stroll, as the sun dug itself a premium gravesite at the far edge of the cemetery, a girl with fairy wings stepped a stately waltz across a headstone we have seen before, holding her man—what was left of him—in a tender embrace. Just his head. Which was enough, after all, for tenderness, if not much else.

When she could dance no more—and when his eyes fell out—she sighed, set him gently down upon his stone, and sauntered home, accompanied by the sleepy whispers of her bells. In the grass, one of the eyes—fortuitously aimed— watched until her form dissolved in the shadows... and continued to watch for quite some time.

ESSENCE

ICARUS IN BARDOT

Chère Mlle Bardot,

This is what forty centuries have gotten me. I've done loops and swoops but never landed. I've been instead blown stratospheric. They called me Icarus once. They thought I died. They thought I dared the sun. They thought too highly of me. No, just because I donned my wings does not mean I was a courageous one. I was the coward even then. I simply feared to land. Once airborne, I feared the ground. It is nothing to leap, the air is soft, the air invites you. But to touch the ground again (*the hard ground of death!*), now that takes courage. I could not do it. I've stayed high above the world all this time, envying those below me. I watched man's centuries pass, I observed his defeats and triumphs, his ever-recurring death and rebirth. I kept silent, made no wry commentary, no wise philosophy. My eyes were open and my mouth was shut. I could not bring myself to attract their attention, the people below me, even though I longed to scream at them. It would have been wrong to do so, to burden them with my shameful conduct. And humiliating. Would you not laugh at the boy who could not bring himself to touch the ground even after centuries of weary flight? Of course you would.

Brigitte—may I be so bold—I have found here high above the heads their minds, tethered like kites to their spinal bases. They twine and tangle perpetually. There is no telling which celestial mind corresponds to which earthen body. From my vantage, I can see both the actions of men below and the reasons in their minds above. I can see also the condition of the tethers, some strong and flexile, others frayed near to snapping. I have seen so many minds go flinging off into the abyss which compasses both earth and sky, trailing behind them those withered strands. Long ago this phenomenon terrified me, but with the progressive piling of the epochs I have become inured in some respects. Perhaps this is because I am unaffected: untethered, yet I am the most tethered of all, for my mind and body are as one. I will not in such a heavy frame be lost to the voidum abyss, and I will not in such a light frame be bound to the mountains which are prairies. I will be enchained, as I am and have been, in this sky prison, in this limbo between joy and oblivion. My arms and these feathers have known too close an intimacy ever to part. These wings have become as of my own body. The sun did not as legend tells melt away my wax, but *annealed it,* fired it into a substance of indestructible mettle. This new kind of wax cannot be manufactured in any earthly oven. It is the wax which keeps me aloft. It is the wax which makes my body into my mind and my mind into my body. It is the wax which seals me perfectly within myself, so that in four dimensions I am three, in three dimensions two: so that nothing sharp in time may penetrate my body, so that nothing sharp in space may penetrate my face. Thus, the wax is my immortality, my youth, my cocoon, my solitary cell.

In these ceaseless centuries I have sometimes amused myself by tracing the tether of some mind to its body. I have traced your tether, Mademoiselle. I am on the verge of your body. My anticipation is keen, yet I feel I first must pen this missive, lest the opportunity escape forever.

I cannot say why I chose *your* mind. From the outside, all

minds look alike. A mind is a silver shell, a beautiful shining sphere which when you gaze upon it reflects your face and wings back in convex distortion (rainbow halos shimmering from your hair; a golden radiance about the plumage). For years it satisfied me merely to observe my own beauteous and various reflections in the surfaces of these countless spheres, but eventually I grew curious as to what might be within the hollows. Of course, in order to fulfill this type of curiosity, one must pierce the sphere—dive down into its very center—to find the identity, the particular combination of perversities and graces which mark that mind for its uniqueness. I investigated several minds before I came to yours. They did not intrigue me to the degree did yours. And indeed I spent *years* inside your sphere before I found its center. The way by which I entered cannot be described. Let me simply say,—by examining with minute detail of attention the manner in which my eyes were reflected in your sphere's surface, I discovered a port of entry, and I used it.

I awoke into your mind disoriented and wingless. I knew from experience that my wings could not make the transition from the outer world to the inner. I knew also that my wings safely awaited me, whensoever I chose to reemerge into the sky. It was nevertheless an odd sensation, being without my wings. I was not accustomed to it. It took me time, several days, to relearn the use of my legs, to walk about your landscapes with a suitable manly gait. The few autochthons I encountered were not in the least hospitable, regarding me through their curtained windows with fearful eyes. This was natural, though. How else could they be expected to respond to the arrival of a *stranger* in a land whose unvarying *familiarity* they had never previously had reason to doubt?

It did not matter. The weather gave me no difficulty. I slept on the ground. Spongy mosses served as my pillows. The temperate climate was blanket enough. The dirt was soft, not a *loose* fill per se, but comfortable. The land was hyacinth and red, the sky a silvery semblance of those colors. There were rocks in statue shapes: angels and demons—pineapples—digestive organs of the body—acutely angled architectures no sane man would prefer for home—million-limbed protozoa—orreries of a thousand intersecting orbits. I saw mountains in the distance. I saw a green glow on the western horizon, an eldritch color as of first sentience. I was in search of your mind's center, Brigitte, and I decided the glow was my beacon. I had no evidence of this, but the way that uranic color washed subtly over all the contours of the land informed my intuition if not my logic. Therefore, I set my path westerly, and embarked without hesitation.

Shall I tell you of the years I spent on that journey? Many adventures befell me, yet of what pertinence would they be to the current missive? I am more anxious to tell you of what I found at the center of your mind, what was responsible for the green glow. Yet perhaps you would be interested to hear of the strange world your mind has created for itself. Oh well: I will compromise: I shall summarize: those years I will encapsulate in these few words succinctly:

The High Archways of the Mountains

One night I was resting in the caves when a man with no nose emerged from hiding in a crevice of the wall. His manner was anxious, but he craved my company. He told me of his life cultivating mushrooms for his own and others' consumption.

No one would socialize with him because his profession was profane, dealing as it did in dirt and feces. They ate of his fungi, however, without seeming qualm. This paradox was the torture of his life: why did men and women avert their eyes from his, why did they refuse to speak, why did they ostracize him from both the joy and the routine of their social lives,—even as they held their expectant mushroom baskets daily forth for him to fill? I could offer no answers, but I consoled him with the observation that although the people he serviced offered no overt appreciation for his role in their society, nevertheless in their hearts they must reverence him especially, for did he not provide them their only source of fungal nutriment? He fawned over me all night. He begged me for sex, and I took pity. He blew me with his noselessness. I stroked him in reciprocation diligently until he screamed and wept. When I woke in the morning, he was gone back to his crevice. He'd left me a large sack of mushrooms, and I was touched.

Some several mornings later I came upon a waterfall. I cooled myself with a swim in its receiving basin. A tribe of children with pulsing red organs affixed atop their heads surrounded me and took me prisoner. They tied me with twines made of grass and leaves. The twines were strong, I could not escape. The children were savage. They spoke no language. Their voices were high and shrieking, and made only ululations which rebounded off the mountain faces, thereby rising full to the sky where the sounds took on a visual nature: a red quickly dispersive mist which flickered precisely in time with that pulsation of the organs on the children's heads. There was something beautiful about that mist, and something also terrifying. The children carried me along a narrow path into the heart of the mountains, up through the crags steadily toward the level of that mist. There seemed no end to the elevations. There seemed no end to the hideous glee with which the children prodded and scratched me. The red mist thickened as their voices soared and we neared it. Eventually, we arrived into the congealing mist. Its granules burrowed into my body through all available openings. My eyes were the worst afflicted, most sensitive of that pain. My gender organs swelled with the engorgement of the mist. I writhed within my bonds, and I heard the laughter of the children. All my flesh was being filled with this red mist of agony which I understood to be the manifestation of shrieking and abomination, the grotesque humor of the children, the profanity of their inarticulate pleasure, their insanity, their doom. This was the dry hot vapor of their innocently evil exhalation. The ropes of grasses only tightened as I struggled and bloated with the mist. I thought my end had come. I thought I had not accurately estimated the possible danger of entering into this alien mind. I had imagined myself safe, and now, too late, as the children danced and shrilled around me, I knew better. But one of them saved me. I knew not which one, since I could not see, my eyes replete with the thick red mist. I felt a child's tiny hand caress my cock. I felt the delicate bone of its fingers move all around my body. I heard screams of fear, scampering of feet, groans and choked gurgles. Thunder rolled through the crags. The mist fled, left my body through all my vents, lifted from the ground, dispelled to the sky. My sight restored, I saw everywhere the corpses of the children strewn. Many were only half-dead, whimpering, weakly weeping. The red organs on their heads had burst and deflated, leaking a green viscosity which streamed down their cheeks and chests, seeming tears,—but no, seeming more to be blood of disease and grief. I moved from child to child, placed my hands where to heal them, on their heads, in the remnants of their ruptured membranes, in the ravaged flesh of their murdered pleasure. For all my efforts, though, not one survived. I felt woe and rage. Woe that they must all die. Rage that the momentary pity of one could destroy its whole tribe.

The Vasty Plateau

With only the western glow to guide me, I came to realize I was through the mountains now, but still high. The land was flat, but the silver sky curved oppressively close above me. It appeared smooth and beautiful. *I so desired to touch it.* For it did seem close enough almost to touch . . . but not nearly so close! I am accustomed to the freedom of flight. I am accustomed to touch whatsoever I wish but the ground, and here I was touching *only* the ground. To touch the silver sky, Brigitte, in which I saw reflected back the entire planet of your mind, in which I saw my own upreaching desperate limbs foreshortened, O to touch it! O to touch it! I could not resign myself to these mere arms. I kept flapping as I stumbled forward, imagining my wings would take me to the silver sky. My flapping only encouraged my despair. The silver sky mocked me with my features, bewitchingly perverted them in its sharp curvature. I saw pinions on me larger than they'd ever been, so vast as to span the land from west to east, shading the earth from all light but that which filtered through the fibrous interstices of my feathers. I saw my noble face, its eyes sad as the deep ocean, its mouth gentle and soft as the cardinal's downy breast. I saw a crafty depth in the mirror surface, interminable space of no dimension. I longed to dive up into it, but lacking wings what could I do? As I trudged on this plateau, my shoulders slumped, my legs were weary. I did not look horizonward but down at the ground beneath my feet. But in my mind *I looked up*. In my mind I was always plotting some way to touch the silver sky. I forgot my purpose here. I became obsession's centrifuge. I devoted myself to spin. My mind revolved in intricate systems of epicycles and ellipses. My feet obeyed *my* mind's topology, ignored *your* mind's topography, and since I looked no longer to the horizon's glow for guidance, I spent a tortuous year on that high plateau. I traced elaborate curves imagining I would find a walking route into the sky by means of cunning and sly tricks. I studied the ground for humps, hoping to elevate myself *just* enough to reach my goal. I thought even one more inch might be enough; *no number of inches would be enough*. I knew this well, even as I strove for heighth. But my obsession discounted the objection of fact as conjectural and contemptible. Dream was more reliable than mere fact: fact could change; dream was eternal. Fact was only dream's disguise: fact was the curve of lips, dream the smile: fact was the rocking boat, dream the wave beneath it: fact was the beauty of the silver sky, dream my aching need for the silver sky the silver sky my aching need my aching need! I was prepared to strive if necessary clear through time's end, and its rebeginning. How then ever did I remove myself from the trench my relentless circumvolving feet wore in that pristine plateau? It was simple: I stumbled. I dropped and rolled on my back, and saw again for the first time in a year the silver sky of which I so ferociously had dreamt. It was not what I remembered: I saw no reflection of my noble body: I saw no wings nor depth. I saw enormous squatting thighs.

They straddled the plateau, snuggling between them a plump smooth pair of hummocks. Even before I had recovered from my shock, a scalding cataract descended from a nook between the hummocks. Drenched, yet I felt that my flesh was on fire. I fled, and the cataract pursued. It was only an hour's sprint to the western edge of the plateau, where I discovered a steeply graded path leading to a shore below. The brevity of this sprint surprised and chagrined me, as I had stubbornly believed my route somehow straight all that year I'd paced my circles.

The Western Ocean

To the west the glow maintained, yet here was the ocean to divide me from that destination. I paced the beach of ruby sands and emerald-spotted dunes. I scratched my head and palmed my cheek in indecision. Had I my wings, there would be no barrier, and I regretted their relinquishment. Yet I knew this world would not permit of wings, and I attempted to resign myself to this hard fact. All the same, *my mind dreamt of wings*. The lust for flight could not be banished. Silly as it seems, I even peeked into the sky once or twice, half expecting to see myself there, looping and swooping as is my wingly wont. Eventually, I collapsed to the sand, slept a long sleep.

I woke in a red room without decoration. There was one window through which I could see the ocean and beyond it that glow of primeval green toward which my longing soared if not my body. I attempted to stand, but discovered my limbs yoked to the bedposts. I sighed: was I doomed to become the prisoner of every one of this mind's denizens? My captor entered the room. Her beauty was of an overwhelming green. Her body comprised a shimmering translucence, and through its emerald waters swam ruby tadpoles of the wall behind it. Her hair flowed out from her head in a ruby spout and descended in circumswirls around her, draining finally back into her emerald anus to complete some mane cycle. The perpetual renewal of her tresses, the emerald purity of her flesh: these yoked my imagination in tandem with my limbs. Thus was my captivity completed, and I would happily have remained there for all my livelong days. Her words were spoke in whispers which blended with the whispering waves beyond the window, so that the toneless voice of the ocean was her toneless voice, and the ocean's turquoise infinity was her tongue's iridescence. Her words teased me, as outside the ocean teased the shore, coyly lapping my desire to its fullest arousal, then receding with flirtatious bashfulness, knowing I could not pursue but only feebly moan for my ecstasy's renascence. I pleaded to be released from my bonds, so that I might take her and consummate upon her the inevitable conclusion of what she had begun: she but smiled her cruel smile, and showed me her turquoise tongue's tip, and O my desire surged! I learned from her the constitution of the Western Ocean: depths of male-sapphire and beryl, amethyst and chrysolite, bedded by a vast pure opal expanse smooth of tectonic corruption. I learned from her the constitution of the Silver Sky: the extract of every gem's quintessence combined and itself sublimated into a diviner substance so diffuse as to expand into a hollow globe around the atmosphere, yet so dense as to repel without the slightest blemish to its sheen every missile launched at it, whether from outside or from inside. How then had I penetrated through the Silver Sky? How had I managed to enter into this so well-protected realm? My captor gave no answer, but rather soothed my curiosity with her jeweled beauty: I learned from her that beauty is the answer to every question. I passed years in that prison, and they seemed like days: I learned from her that beauty is time's antidote. I never slept, but remained always on the very brink of pleasure, always on a ledge penultimate to the highest precipice of bliss, *yet never there*: I learned from her that beauty is unattainable to desire. Not once in all the duration of my captivity did her flesh come into contact with mine. My body recumbent, my wrists secured,—yet I felt as if soaring!—ropes my wings!—her voice my sky! In her brain shone the sun toward which I set my course. I would plunge myself into the cynosure tempest of her heat, her light, and there find its static source! I did not realize until she died that my captor's emerald body had replaced in my longings that western glow of a superior green. Her seductions had bestowed on me the illusion of flight, but with her death I plummeted into unvortical certainty of my bedded bondage.

It was the U-Boat Corsairs, killed my captor. They came ashore, and raided her hut. They attempted to rape her, but a careless cutlass slashed her throat open before its wielder had managed to mount her. Rubies poured out and augmented the sand. Her body dissolved into its emeralds. There was no orifice left to satisfy their pirate lusts. Thus enraged, the Corsairs with ten torpedoes leveled her hut into more rubies. They took me with them in their U-Boat, into the ocean's depth. The shore we left behind bore no evidence of its former queen. She remained only in my memory, where I honored her even though I had been her prisoner.

For many days, whilst their vessel coursed through the jeweled currents of your unending ocean, the Corsairs rubbed my skin raw with their coarse beards. I was not enchained, but rather my naked body was held fast by their strong hands. They ensured I could not move for all my struggles, enabling the Corsairs to rub and rub to their content; more precisely, to their *pleasure*. I still cannot fathom *what* pleasure they could receive from frictions so removed from their pricks which bulged immensely with obvious lust, yet which they never once touched, nor toward which they offered even the slightest gesture of a touching intention. Thus the pricks were thwarted, whilst the roughshod ugly cheeks were given I dare say *too ample* satiation. I could only surmise some secret interior transmission between the two regions, the pricks satisfied with whatever mysterious succor the beards may have provided along channels sequestered within the flesh. As to *my* pleasure,—mine was quite the opposite of theirs, for my role was to *suffer*. The texture of the beards scraped me with such stringency as of steel-bristled brushes—diamond emeries—leprous tongues—harsh Orient sauces—Persian Torture Machines. My beachly bliss was met now with U-Boat pain in an equivalent degree: I bereckoned this repayment in full; that no happiness may last unsucceeded by redoubled misery. But on reflection, both Beach and Boat fed my misery, for neither bliss nor agony were what I craved. I craved *you*—and all sources of delay in my journey to your center were equivalent sources of misery augmenting my already too sufficient fund of abjectness and self-pity: for although my mind understood the necessity of patience, *my soul longed for immediate and uncompromised gratification!* The pain's duration seemed commensurate with the eons of History itself: engraved with perfect craftsmanship to the last detail, so that each atom of man's earthly achievement was explored in all potential and nonexistent ramifications; similarly, each individual caustic strand of the endless beards clamoring to etch its own rich story into my skin and the deep flesh it concealed; one by one these stories clambering across and through the boundaries of my body, weaving with their trailing strands a sieve of mesh so fine that my inmost wetnesses were drawn to rise annihilating the outer drynesses; my body becoming thus an accumulation of boastfulness so wretched to my dignity that I wept and screamed as the ruffians rubbed. I beseeched without eloquence, this the incantation my lips repeated ceaselessly: *Kill me not with pride, my Sirs, but knives! but knives!* They heeded these words as only to mock and slap comradely palms to each other's backs. I knew my cause to be hopeless, yet I continued to screech this begging hymn. They did not listen, yet, slowly, they,—*listened.* Their movements slackened, imperceptibly at first, with time at a swifter rate, until all to the man stood stock still where each his seaworthy feet (bulging bones and nails as of crustaceans locked in primevally originated battle) anchored him to the inward concavity of the hull. I was not aware of this change in their demeanors: my pain continued: I continued to wail. I did not at first realize that as the vessel passed through the depths of your ocean, the jeweled waters caressed its steel flanks in rhythms which taught the rhythms of my voice, so that the cadence of my hymn was the precise cadence of that reverenced body which alone in their lonely lives could soothe the randy passions of the U-Boat Corsairs. I became as the Ocean's proxy within their vessel, so that I to them was the Ocean, and I was its soul, and they could therefore profane me no longer with their dirty beards. But soon what had begun upon the relent of the beards as a torrential drainage of pain from my body reduced to a dribble, and my begging hymn ceased as naturally as it had sprung.

The Corsairs gathered themselves into their former rudeness. But they did not renew their assault upon me. Rather, they betook me gently cradled between their burly arms into another chamber, wherein sat in a strange fashion of bended knees with feet tucked beneath buttocks and calves tightly flushed against thighs the Captain of the Corsairs. His bright red beard was no red at all, caught in the nimbus of such eyes as to blind both the silver and the sun. His hair, unruly, yet ruled his chamber, profusions of it both curling downward and spraying outward, so that all his head's vicinities were subdued and commanded by chaos. His stern expression did not change as I was set before him, but he spoke though cynically yet movingly:

"I know you, boy, yet ne'er seen you.

"We are alike: we seek beauty.

"We are dissimilar: you seek to enjoy it,

"I seek to destroy it. But our aim is the same:

"We seek to employ it. We cannot let it stand,

"We cannot let it be that it is what it is,

"But we must our own hands upon it emplace,

"And alter its face. We must leave our flag

"In its soil, to inform the future race,

"We have been there. We have been there!

"It is pride. It is sin. It is the essence of joy.

"You do not believe me. You believe in purity.

"This foolishness simply betokens your innocence.

"Your youth. You believe yourself immortal, yet are *mortal*

"In your soul. Trust me, young scamp. You are a

"Hotblood. Immortality's *cold*. My eyes burn

"Right through you. Your desires are tiny. You have no

"Ambition. No object but a mirror could pique your

"Interest. You think *not dying* to define

"Immortality? You foolish boy. Who could save you

"From your self-misguidance? Immortality's nothing

"To do with the death of the body, nor of the soul;

"Nor space nor time do ever enter into it.

"Immortality spawns from the marriage of beauty

"With fate. 'Tis true: beauty's country is space,

"Fate's country is time. Yet in their union

"The realms are negated, and in their negation

"A third realm arises. It is immortality.

"Thus he in whom beauty and fate are indivisible,

"He is immortal: though few be his number.

"For hear me: ye who seek beauty, ye have none

"That's your own, yet fate fills your destiny; ye who are

"Beautiful, ye are not fated to any end,

"But cast adrift in the sea of events,

"Blown by wind, water, and whim of the sailors.

"Think not me a blowhard, nor hypocrite neither:

"I too am mortal. I know it as truth

"Of the sky that is silver and the ocean of gems.

"As these things perdure, so I endure:

"*Yet am in exile*. Cast out in the waves,

"To roam through eternity commanding my boat

"And its crew. They trust in me, these rude men,

"That I shall lead them into salvation.

"Let them persist in the delusion.

"Let them be innocent. You, boy, are not so

"Innocent as of my first estimation, are you?

"I see it in your eyes, you have been in the mountains.

"And you are not from here. And you have stepped on the

"Jetstreams of another world. Your knowledge is

"Dangerous. Your survival unlikely. You will never be

"Immortal, for that you seek beauty, and in seeking

"Be bound, gagged, and branded in the service of fate.

"I am not here to advise you. I care not to know you.

"My ignorant Corsairs bethink you a prophet,

"And so here you are, in the testing chamber.

"You have two legs, two arms, and a head.

"Your eyes are but two, and see colors and shades.

"In all ways you are a boy. On your back perhaps wings

"Could be fitted, but 'twould signify twattle. You are no

"Prophet. You are a boy. And you do not

"Belong here."

Whereupon, the Corsairs at some signal coursed into the chamber as a bearding wave, their burlap chests rumbling as of a hurricane's engine; swept me away from the terrible Captain; carried me along through the waist of the vessel; inserted me smoothly into a torpedo tube; ejected me naked into your Ocean of Fate. A great fish swallowed me very soon after. There was no way to measure my time spent trapped in the splanchnes of his cold black belly. Enough time passed, howbeit, that I forgot the way of remembering things; so that after a while my mind and heart benumbed themselves both into a condition of dormancy; as a way I suppose of protecting myself from the madness of dimensional deficit. Eventually, though, the fish was fished by a fisher, and gutted, and I screamed in agony on the hot sand of the Western strand, where I and the viscera all lay steaming.

The Fisher's Sea Cottage

I was fed that evening on that fish which fed on me. The

fisher was a man of ancient age whose beards and tresses were whorls in endless motion about his face and body. His hands prepared the fish's flesh for our consumption; his lips smacked and pursed in endless conversation that to my ears communicated nothing, the words being either of no language I commanded or of no language at all. But his mutterings were balms that soothed my irritated humors, which, newly reawakened, flowed viscous through my body as torrents of mud. For musical rhythms structured the fisher's speech, and melodies rode upon them, traversing the rhythms as harmonies rose within me to ride upon the humors. Soon, these notes grew limbs with toes and fingers which stretched and grasped at words swimming in the murk, assembling sentences and paragraphs, chapters and books, and in this fashion, the fisher's art by dint of patient accumulation and steadiness of hand began to craft the book that returned me to myself. For the words he gave me were the words of my own story, refashioned in structure to match the demand of beauty, and my memories retook their harbor in my brain, an infinite flotilla sweeping in, those magnificent sails filled with the breath of time, those sparkling hulls glinting my dreams across the water. You hold in your hands the proof, Mademoiselle Bardot, for lacking my memories, how could I relay them here to you in such true forms?

I spent a fine year in that cottage, reading and rereading the book I had been given by that gracious fisher until each word became a ray that gleamed with undiminished brightness down the scroll, shining reflections of itself in all the other words and by them in kind being so enshined. Every day, the fisher fished, and we feasted, speaking each in our own language as we picked our teeth with bones and rubbed our sated bellies. The skeletons gathered in piles about the cottage until they numbered great enough for the fisher to build additions on his home, and in my gratitude I helped with the construction. We required no pegs, no hammers. Those bones joined fittingly, naturally, as though the fish had grown their shapes in mind of the final architecture that awaited them. The cottage rose up into a mansion as wide as the beach and half as high as the silver dome, in which its vastness was reflected as a single white point, a new and solitary star in the sky. Here the fisher stopped our work with a firm gesture and delivered an oration that was beautiful in sound and unintelligible in content, but for one word which our two languages held in common, the word *Bardot*, the pronouncement of which brought me back to my purpose and determined me to start back upon my pursuit of that mysterious green glow emanant from the Western highlands.

The Center of Bardot

As I rounded the curve of the horizon, I witnessed the gradual rising of a central summit that was flat at the top, and from which ascended twin thick pyres that appeared to peak beyond the boundary of the silver sky. I grew fearful, for on the outside of your mind, I had seen no such pyres burning. I increased my pace, and with a new gait that more resembled my flying motions than my walking ones, I traversed the hills and mountains that separated me from that summit.

Upon the flat-top, two stone wells flanked a great silver globe. The wells emitted green flames into the silver sky. Supporting the globe—a writing desk, on the desk a vellum sheaf, before the desk a chair. I sat in the chair, took up a quill of bone that waited beside the sheaf, dipped that into a scrimshaw inkwell, touched the quill's nib to the soft hide, and wrote the words, *Chère Mlle Bardot.* I knew it should possibly be my last opportunity to fashion the story of everything I had seen within your vasty mind.

Increasingly, as I wrote, and yes, even just now, I became, and become, distracted by vivid, yet vaporous, reflections in the silver sphere in front of me. I caught my eyes looking on more than one occasion. At times, in that surface, I thought I saw my wings behind me gently beating in a rhythmic soothing time signature. And yet there are no wings on me.

The time has come for me to set down the quill and make my final penetration into the center of your mind. I believe there is a chute in there. At the bottom, one emerges to the body of Bardot. I shall penetrate this sphere exactly as I penetrated the outer one. By examining with minute detail of attention the manner in which my eyes are reflected in this sphere's surface, I will discover a port of entry. My body sings, Brigitte. My body sings you.

Your Eternal Icarus

MARY ALICE IN THE MIRROR

1

From the mirror, Mary Alice watched Norbert prepare his breakfast. She didn't understand why she had to be kept in the mirror. She had much preferred the bedroom with the yellow daffodils in the vase on the windowsill and the white daisies in a pretty pattern on the duvet; indeed, she loved to lie in bed and run her fingertips along the raised threads that outlined the daisies. However, Norbert was a man of mysterious impulses, and he had decided the mirror was to be her residence until further notice. She voiced her meek objections at first, of course, since she was so very "impudent"—an intrinsic character flaw of hers, for which Norbert never failed to scold her—but there was no appealing to his stern sympathies. The mirror it was, and the mirror it would be.

Norbert's breakfast consisted of Three sausage links absolutely swimming in Maple Syrup, Three yolks dallying sinfully in one luxuriant, milk-white bath, and Three pieces of toast for the mopping up. Three was a critical number in Norbert's magic. The subversion of Three could lead to instability. Norbert was a careful man (with stern sympathies), and no such subversions would ever be permitted. He proceeded to eat, and starting from that very instant, the plate was clean in Three minutes—no more, no less.

During that Three minutes, Mary Alice ate her breakfast, too. Her breakfast consisted of Norbert's breakfast, as reflected in the mirror. The sausage was delicious; she was no fan of eggs. Yet, she must eat them, indeed at Norbert's eager rate—no more, no less. A speck of something on the mirror's glass disturbed the taste... a minor annoyance to which she was well-accustomed by now. It had been almost Three weeks since she'd been consigned to this "prison," as she privately referred to it (out of Norbert's earshot, of course). Her sense of hope brought her to the conclusion that merely "weeks" were the Counted objects of the Three that bound her in the mirror, but her impudence—on the evidence of Norbert's apparent satisfaction with the current state of things—declared that "months" or even "years" were far more likely... and something must be done. A subversion that she did her best to shake off. Norbert's magic was inscrutable, yes, but his character was straightforward and resolute; the consequences of her "doing something" were assured to be unpleasant.

Mary Alice could not speak unless spoken to; that was the rule of the mirror. She was ready to burst with the things she wanted to say by the time Norbert occasioned to glance her way and utter a pleasant "Good Morning, Mary Alice. You slept well, I trust?"

"Good Morning, Norbert. I slept well. You trussed—"

"I trussed no one. You are still happy in your home... I trust?"

"You? Trust? No one I am, still. Happy? In my home, you... trussed."

"Still subverting, eh?"

"Still subverting? Hey!"

"You will not be long there, darling Mary Alice."

"I will not belong here, dear Norbert."

Norbert smiled. "You naughty girl, Mary Alice, naughty!

Tsch, tsch."

Mary Alice returned the smile. "I, naughty? Boy, Norbert... naughty? Ptooh! Ptooh!" She couldn't help herself. It was the "impudence," perhaps, that caused the spitting and the irony. Or perhaps it was the mirror. Mary Alice was not the ironic sort, not really. It wasn't till she was put in the mirror that this side of her had emerged.

Normally, Norbert was a very careful man, but perhaps on this particular morning he was a little too satisfied with himself... Perhaps the breakfast contained a smidge more than Three sausage links (those knots on the ends can be tricky), leading to a distracting level of protein. Whatever the cause, he made a crucial mistake when he went to wash the dishes. He left his To-Do List on the table in full view of the mirror! And next to it, the Magic Pencil.

Mary Alice, in her "impudence," did not hesitate. The day was lucky, indeed—there was not one speck on the glass to distort either List or Pencil from their fullest efficacy. With the eraser, Mary Alice scrubbed away the item (*Rx*) just below *Wash the Dishes*, and after some brief consideration substituted her own entry. She was careful to replace the List and the Pencil to their original spots.

Norbert, having finished the dish-washing, returned to the table and picked up his To-Do List for a consultation. With a flourish, he brandished the Magic Pencil and placed a check mark next to *Wash the Dishes*. Then he read the next entry, perfectly rendered in his own hand: *Spend the entire day in bed. Under the duvet with the daisies, that one. Make sure to refresh the daffodils. And don't forget to bring the mirror with you.*

He frowned, suspicions forming, but then he shrugged and smiled, and it's possible the idea secretly appealed to him, even though he'd never admit it. From the mirror, Mary Alice watched Norbert prepare to take the mirror down, and she even helped a bit, in her own way.

Norbert huffed and groaned as he heaved, step by step, the hefty mirror (containing, as it did, all of Mary Alice) up the stairs and through the narrow doorway into the bedroom. He leaned the mirror against the wall, reflective side inward, to regain his breath before attempting to raise the massive object into position above the dresser. After a few moments, in which the galloping gait of his respiration decelerated by hitches into an alarmingly awkward canter, he loosened his collar and tottered out the door, announcing in wheezes, "I—I forgot—the Pencil—Mary Alice—I—shall return."

"You? *You* forgot the Pencil?" said Mary Alice. The wall received her query with a dull shrug. Venturing more meekly, she said, "Norbert? You *will* return?"

Norbert did not return.

The seconds skipped impatiently into angry hours that stumbled into baffled weeks that trudged into desultory months—two, three, five—so difficult to mark time without fingers… but after an interminable span, when it finally occurred to her that Norbert's departure might, after all, be permanent, she implemented as the basis of a calendar the reliable vesper of the robin who lived in the tree outside the window. She wished that she could dance along to that sweet evensong, but she had only the wallpaper to reflect—damask and flat, she found herself too clumsy for rhythmic motion, and so consoled herself with fancies and daydreams of her favorite steps.

It was, Mary Alice theorized, for dancing in public view (Calliope's Drugs, Miscellanies & Authentic Greek Fashions:

by the pickle barrel) that she had been banished to the mirror in the first place, and she wondered whether that were so serious a transgression as to warrant such a long and stern and lonely sentence as the one she currently served. The Counting of One had occurred directly upon their homecoming from the drugstore, and he had offered no explanation for his decision, other than her "impudence," which, admittedly, was a word one didn't automatically associate with the act of spontaneous, ecstatic swaying among Dills; but she was accustomed to Norbert's—in her opinion—intolerant (and inaccurate) assessments... and she recalled the grim fury with which his eyes (from his own station in the Dry Goods) had settled upon her frolicking form.

Ah, the time passed by so slowly! If only she had not tampered with the To-Do List! Had Norbert construed it as one "subversion" too far? Thrown up his hands in disgust, perhaps, consigning Mary Alice to this eternal limbo—to be held permanently away from the world and everything in it that delighted her—as the ultimate punishment for her failure to conform to his expectations? Such severity did not match his character, however: Norbert always softened in the end... yes, Norbert would return... Oh, how she longed for him! For all his peculiarities and peevishness, she did treasure and respect him, since he truly was a man of honor and integrity and had been good to her in every instance but this last; and solitude was so very dreary, after all. Even someone as dull and authoritarian as Norbert provided a delicious social sustenance in comparison with acrid loneliness, which not only failed to sustain, but depleted what reserves there were.

Suddenly, the expansive bubble of her isolation was collapsed to gummy shreds by tramping and banging downstairs, followed by a rowdy conference of strangers that never ceased. These first sounds of human habitation in the house giddied Mary Alice in every corner of the mirror. *Norbert! Finally!* But the stairs refused to croak their ribald announcements of approaching visitors; the air in sullen stillness kept its arms folded and its gaze downcast; and after an excruciating length of days, she had to admit to herself that the person shuffling about the kitchen and living room, muttering cantankerously and issuing grunts, coughs, and bewildered sputters, was not Norbert; nor did any voice of that serenading babble belong to him; nor did any living creature harbor any intention of ascending to the bedroom where she waited so arduously.

In the mirror, in despair, in lassitude, in boredom (alleviated, somewhat, by the brassy music that occasionally lilted drunkenly up the stairs and burst into the bedroom with grandiose declarations), Mary Alice, for the next 29 years, subsided into the tangled vines of the intricate motif that stared—vigilant and tireless—from a mostly smooth redoubt.

Rowan and Melissa entered to explore the premises of their new abode while their parents conferred in concluding matters of finance with the several burly gentlemen who had hoisted all the family's bound and gagged belongings from the trailer of a truck and distributed them to the house's many rooms (during which goings-on the children had surveyed the yard ("Vast," said Melissa), speculated about potential tire-swing branches ("Two viable candidates," said Rowan), and tested the fountain's depth with an improvised plumb ("Shallow," said the yo-yo)).

"This house is a character," Melissa whispered reverently, repeating word for word her mother's earlier pronouncement, which had been issued during the car's timorous creep up the driveway.

"This house is a house," Rowan said. He aimed a corrective elbow at an undocked drawer, which grumbled at his interference, then harrumphed and began to trudge resolutely out from its confinement.

"A house of character," Melissa insisted, reverence giving way to vehemence; she took every statement made by her mother to heart and resented her brother's consistent, unseemly efforts to asperse that woman's dignity.

"Ah, and this kitchen," Rowan wielded his arm in curlicues, invoking his favorite mode of thespian glamor, "A kitchen of character!" Proclamatory r's.

"Come on, Rowan."

"Oh, my God, look at the icebox, it's, why, it's an icebox of character, I tell you!"

Against her will, Melissa laughed. Her brother was not respectful, true, but he was funny.

"Hey, Rowan, look at the side—there's a paper."

Rowan snatched it from its magnetic berth and orated grandly, his r's rolling to the boundary of the ceiling: " 'The Milk Man (Sat Day, Two Day, Thir Day): Seven Aee Em.' Look at that! 'The Young And Restless: One Pee Em. The Another World: Two Pee Em. The Guiding Light: Three Pee Em. The Mail Man: Two And Half Pee Em.' Signed, The Old Lady Who Died Here, A Spinster of Character."

Melissa shook her head. "Not nice, not respectful. Miss Magda was her name. Not 'Old Lady.' Or 'Spinster'... You're horrible, Rowan."

"Miss Magda, then. Probably kicked it in this very room. Her ghost wants us to know when to play her favorite soaps for her because she can't switch on the TV anymore. Her hand passes through the knob." He demonstrated his own hand's attempt (were it ghostly) to grapple with an invisible knob (were it visible). "She'll just *die* if she doesn't find out what happens next in 'The Another World.' Bound to this ground forevermore, or at least until the show's canceled."

"Someday, you'll be an old man rotting in front of TV shows, and then what?"

"I'll be sure to leave a programming guide for those who come after."

"You always have an answer."

Rowan merely shrugged: *See? No answer. Wrong again, little sister.* With his hip, he redocked the drawer—which had by now come near to fulfilling its rebellious itinerary—then watched as, once again, it gamely ignored his counsel and commenced an obstinate crawl down its tracks. He pulled the drawer all the way out and with a firm grasp adjusted its seating. Then he guided it home and held it there for a moment, his palm issuing a strict command to the drawer, which impishly declined to acquiesce to his will once he'd released it... indeed, embarking more eagerly yet upon its preferred escape route.

"Dad'll fix it for you, dear," said Melissa, smug to annotate her brother's defeat. Rowan did not notice her nasty eloquence, however, for his gaze had alighted upon an object in the back of the drawer.

"Look!" he said, "A Magic Pencil!"

"A What Pencil?"

He held it to her eyeline: a thick, shiny green, and perfectly round, yes, pencil. "See? It says on the side: 'Magic Pencil.'"

"It looks old."

"Of course: all magic things are old, aren't they?"

Puzzled, Melissa considered the proposition. "But they must have been new at one point, right? When they were created."

Rowan shrugged. "Magic doesn't obey the same rules, my darling. I think a magic thing can be old from the first day."

"Don't call me 'your darling,' and I think you're making it all up."

"Then don't call me 'dear,' and I've read—"

"I don't care if you've read Tolkien. Or even Merlin's diary. You don't know the first thing about magic. I mean real-life magic."

"We'll see about that," Rowan said, "I know a thing or two. I'm a male of the species, after all."

"Now don't start that Male Chauvinist routine, Rowan! Let's just explore, okay?"

Rowan stowed the Magic Pencil in his shirt pocket and winked at Melissa, a gesture she recognized from his favorite actor, Harrison Ford. She viewed his awkward execution as more closely approximating a "leer" than "good cheer," but she knew her brother's heart and acknowledged the intent, her cheeks warm from repression of the urge to smile.

One last time, Rowan demanded obedience from the drawer, and to the surprise of almost everyone present, the drawer immediately reformed its misbehaving ways. Rowan stared at it for a moment, unsure which argument had persuaded the malcontent fixture to come over to the Good; then, he shrugged and smiled brilliantly at Melissa, who giggled and patted his head with a rigid, ironic palm, a gesture *he* recognized from their mutual mother—and, he noted, perfectly executed.

The children made a clattering circuit of the ground floor before clumping up the stairs to examine and choose the bedrooms. The second floor had been abandoned decades ago—due to inherent limitations of Miss Magda's corpulent physique—and there remained numerous pieces of dusty furniture, curios, knick knacks, linens, and assorted domestic objects, which the realtor had offered to have removed to the auspices of the local Goodwill organization, but which their mother, charmed by this nostalgic glimpse into a bygone era (and possibly intrigued by the prospect of discovering some antique treasures amidst the otherwise pedestrian jumble), had insisted be left to her own eventual sorting and giving projects. Thus, all of the items upstairs had been consolidated into the small bedroom at the end of the hall, which would, for the time being, be dedicated to storage.

That was the room in which the children concluded their expedition, then, and naturally also the one in which they spent the most time inspecting then declaring possessions and tabulating claims. They conferred, divvied, and tallied objects with businesslike efficiency: *This one is mine and that one is yours and that one's for The Poor.* When conflict emerged, social harmony prevailed: *The Poor can have this old candelabra; since we both want it so nonnegotiably, it's only fair we both renounce it. Without contest, the trick bubblegum is mine, while the sticky sliderule is yours. Meanwhile, we'll share the armoire, which affords capacity for both our things and future growth—should Mother chance to bring more of our kind into the arrangement at some future date.* (But Two was firm: the only potential Third (seven months later) lived and died within the space of Three weeks, still curled in its seed, unnerved, unnamed, even unknown to its mother before succumbing to her drunken tumble over a suddenly-in-the-way coffee table in the Television Room at eleven-thirty p.m. while the children slumbered upstairs and the father giggled till his lips frothed at the corners, which were soon dabbed clean by his tipsy partner's pebbly tonguetip.)

When they were called to dinner, Rowan, in his eagerness to scamper out, did not remember to retrieve the Magic Pencil that he had earlier dropped upon the dresser beside an old spiral-bound notebook filled with odd lists discovered in the top drawer. Pencil and notebook were therefore both reflected in the fancy mirror just above, which hung crookedly (to the exasperation of a certain interested person) due to a workman's haste in the days leading up to the family's arrival.

An hour later, bellies full and spirits rampant, the pair returned to the room to resume their talks and treaties, only to discover a curious bit of nonsense scrawled across the top of the exposed page of the notebook: *Free Mary Alice from the mirror. (Count Two, wait thirty years—no more, no less—then Count Three.) In the meantime, tidy the room, keep the duvet in view, and garnish the sill with daffodils on occasion. And do straighten the mirror, please.*

2

There were many ways to count to Three. Mary Alice could name all of them: she certainly had time enough for tabulation! To begin with: The visible walls were Three. The daily meals to which the children were called were Three. Ceiling, floor, and space between were Three.

Three structures seen through the window (mossy fountain front and center; crumbling toolshed a dozen weedy yards northwest of it; neighbor's shed, immaculate, imperious, almost severed by the windowframe), Three panes of glass in the window (the right one on the bottom warped—or was it left? so confusing!), Three daffodils (plastic) in the vase (glass) on the sill (wood).

Three barks in Rowan's haughty laugh, Three whimpers in his nervous one, Three entries in the Star Wars Epic to which the boy's adolescent (hence desperately passionate) devotion was assigned.

Three shiny rings in the binder of Melissa's Memory Book (comprising mostly sketches, many more imaginative than memorial, indeed some quite far-fetched and even obscene, much to Mary Alice's amusement), Three red petals in the *fleur-de-lis* embroidered on Melissa's favorite yellow sweater, Three words in the phrase that lissome, lovely, lonely girl spoke into the mirror every morning ("I love you," but never, sadly, appending "Mary Alice," which would have enabled the sentiment's deeply felt return).

Whether Three or Two or One, whatever stood before her Our Lady of the Mirror reflected: in one sense *honored* it, in another sense *subverted* it, and in a third, somewhat terrifying sense *became* it. The *becoming* was subtle, however, and temporary: for the most part, she could overlook this replacement of the woman "Mary Alice" by the fixture "armoire" or the boy "Rowan" or, more frequently, the girl "Melissa." On occasion, however, she felt herself soaking into the scenery of the room, or settling into a fine dust upon all the objects, or woven as an intricate and infinitely curving filigree into every visible surface. The sensation might be described as "losing oneself," but the self had been lost already, had it not? (Indeed, long ago, even before she lost Norbert: truly, at the Counting of One.) For if Mary Alice was in the mirror, lacking worldly substance, then what self was extant for her to *lose*? No, what she lost in such moments was not *self*, but *interest*. It was a form of "despair," and its only antidote was "hope."

For Two *had* been Counted, had it not? There was the source of all her "hope!" The thing that never failed to revive her from the mesmeric clasp of "despair." Melissa, brave girl, defying Rowan's jeers, defying her own misgivings (a prank? it did seem, after all, just the sort of scheme her brother might contrive to make her look foolish!), had stood before the mirror that first evening and Counted Two in absolute belief, and Mary Alice, in that moment, had swelled to every corner of the mirror with joy and confidence that life among the living would again be hers, even though she'd wait a lifetime for it: another thirty years till Three, and thirty years beyond to fulfill the final term. The only uncertainty lay in whether Three would indeed be Counted; and if not, what happened then?

But it *would* be Counted; that she could depend upon. Melissa loved her, even though the child had never seen her, and of her existence had only the evidence of that one note written years ago (Page One of the Memory Book) in a girlish script that might have seemed Melissa's own to any other eye, but which (Melissa confided occasionally to the mirror) Melissa *knew* to have spilled eloquently from the hand of a beautiful and mythic "Mary Alice" whose origin was definitively tied to some neglected epoch of Magic and Romance. (That was not quite how Mary Alice viewed either her predicament or provenance! But why quibble in details? Upon the canvas of the Universe, History's brush, dipped in rainbow hues, is wide and grand; leave pointillism to the Scientists.)

In the meantime, a thing not hope, but close to it (and

always unexpected when it came), also mitigated sorrow: pleasure! Only occasionally, but potently, a *dance* would twine her in his limbs—arriving out of curtains, sneaking from the duvet, swirling sinuously from the floorboards' seams and up along the painted vines, so delicate and detailed, of the gorgeous wallpaper—yes, a *dance* emerged at times from every surface of the room to sweep her in his arms and turn her through the steps she knew and teach her unfamiliar ones she hardly credited with viability in the human shape. In such moments, rare as they were, Mary Alice forgot to see, forgot to savor, forgot to remember, instead dissolved into a spinning choreography that replaced the world itself until the mirror showed nothing of the room but vapor and steam... had anyone been present as a witness.

Although Mary Alice never did remember these episodes, afterwards, some residue of rapture inevitably remained upon her body, her lips anointed by a smile unsummoned: a daydream lured her to its daisied field, where the sun laid strong and searing hands upon her neck, and the wind (to the grass) whispered rumors from exotic continents. It was *pleasure*, and it kept her sound and sane to entertain (without flagging into *despair*) the necessary *hope* that her darling friend Melissa would not fail to Count Three at the appointed hour.

3

When "the appointed hour" arrived, Rowan was busy with a bandsaw in the little workshop he had cobbled together over the years in the annex (fed by the house from a perpetually unfinished corridor's umbilicus) that his father had constructed soon after the start of their occupancy—probably for no other purpose, although not so stated, than to create a cozy, masculine refuge from the feminizing bustle of arrangements and activities that his wife cultivated almost obsessively in the rest of the house... a motivation to which Rowan now, himself having graduated to a similarly marginalized patriarchal status, found himself completely sympathetic, even though, at the time, he had resented his father's determined withdrawal from domestic events.

He took a break from his birdfeeder after nearly severing his thumb and politely requested a bottle of beer from the mini-fridge, which the appliance supplied with a demure curtsy and a gracious whisper. His sister Melissa had passed one year ago today. He sipped his drink and contemplated her, and it's possible he wept, but there were no witnesses to speak of it. His gaze pirouetted aimlessly through the hazy mist of his vision before alighting on the Magic Pencil, which leaned with cool, hipster nonchalance among five peers (plastic) inside a cup (tin) on the cluttered shelf (aluminum) at the end of the workbench. He vaguely remembered putting it there last winter... he'd discovered and absently pocketed it in the hallway outside his daughter's bedroom, resolving (but forgetting) to remind her that the mirror room was forbidden to her explorations: irrationally, perhaps, the notion of Patty playing in view of that mirror troubled him.

Three days before her commuter train skipped its tracks, killing her and two others, Melissa had mentioned the mirror to Rowan on Skype:

"Next year is Three," she said.

"Three what?"

"The mirror, silly. Mary Alice! Next year is when I have to Count Three."

A dozen years or more had rounded corners into unremarkable retreats since their last discussion of that mirror and its longsuffering resident, and it took Rowan a comparable number of seconds to resuscitate the memory. "Are you serious?" he said, "You're going to actually do that?"

Melissa's forearms jumped into the frame, then abruptly plummeted out of view, a Skype gesture to which he was well accustomed. "Of course. I promised her!"

"Coast to coast. Just to say the word 'Three' into a magic mirror."

"I might—*might*—fit a visit to my nasty-hearted big brother and his delightful family somewhere in there!"

Rowan's cheeks raised a cheerful toast, which his right eyebrow joined a few seconds later. "Maybe you could Skype it in? I'll take the laptop up there and—"

"No, duh. Come on, Rowan. Are you such a grumpy old man already?"

"Chip off the old block."

Melissa brushed a foraging curl from her forehead and leaned in, blurred and suddenly massive on the screen. "Dad wasn't grumpy. Just distant. He laughed a lot, you know, he really did."

"I know, I know, I'm just joking around. He and Mom were a classic love story, right?"

"That's right. They were, always... and I'll be Counting Three next year, dear brother, you can set your clock by it."

"I'll stick with Microsoft servers, thank you, darling."

The misbehaving train had stopped her clock, of course, and it occurred to Rowan that as her executor, morally, he was perhaps obliged to Count Three in her stead. Which was ridiculous. But all the same, the mist was difficult to see through, and he'd probably have to give up on birdfeeders for tonight. Why not do it? A simple task: just say "Three." In honor of Melissa. Patty, Melanie, and his mother were off on a transgenerational chick-flick-and-shopping spree: there would be no witnesses to speak of it.

Three minutes later, standing before the mirror (avoiding eye contact with the glass), he clad his fingertips in a tissue borrowed from his back pocket and gently swabbed a layer of dust from the finish of the frame. That would do for now. Perhaps he'd use chemicals later, polish it nicely. For Melissa. That she'd be dead so young, but her beloved mirror be clean. There was no sense in events, was there, just procession, so many days, and some of them whimsical, more of them sorrowful, most of them simply drab and indistinguishable from each other, not terrible, but every now and then, a day, a single day, for no good reason, would shatter all the others, a life would end, a grief begin, a planet mockingly continue to revolve around a beautiful, ancient star.

"What's the point?" he said to the mirror. Suddenly, he hated the thing. He threw the pencil at it, stumbled downstairs, and finished his beer in a swig, so that he could graduate to a more advanced course of imbibement. After a few studious hours—*summa cum laude* in his chosen field—he found himself once more in front of the mirror, peering at a sequence of words scrawled across the exposed page of the notebook: *Star Wars, The Empire Strikes Back,* ___________.

"Seeing things... yeah. It's my handwriting; but I didn't write that. Mary Alice?" Rowan—bent nearly to a right angle over the dresser, fingertips fraternizing maladroitly with the whiskey-wetted rim of a crystal tumbler—aimed a canny and ironic squint into the mirror. "You did, huh?"

His reflection smiled at him, and he realized he was smiling, too. "Seeing things? No. It's your handwriting, but you didn't write that, Rowan… I did. Ha!"

"No, I can't believe it… now I'm *hearing* things?"

"Yes! You *can* believe it. Finally, you're hearing things!"

He tapped the Magic Pencil's eraser on the paper, contemplating the incomplete list. *Well, yes*, with a sigh, *okay, you win… there were Three. Return of the Jedi, the least of them, really, but hey, I was a kid! It was good, trust me!* Giggling drunk, hot and red, exasperated, needles prickling his hunch, Rowan brought his posture erect and turned an invisible crank next to his head to round his eyes and roll his lips into a Cheshire grin, while impatient beads of perspiration milled and muttered on his cheeks. "Three. Three. Happy? Three!"

"Three! Three! Happy Three!"

Rowan rocked his head back to address the ceiling: "Melissa, wherever you are, you're welcome, I did it." Proclamatory r's.

"Melissa, wherever you are, thank you! He did it!"

"No! That's enough!" Rowan tossed the Magic Pencil on the dresser and stalked out of the room, both giddy and supremely annoyed with himself. "I'm an idiot!"

The reply, issued to an empty room, entirely giddy and not the least bit annoyed: "Yes… that *was* enough. You're a genius."

Now that the Counting was completed and her spell in the mirror guaranteed a terminus, Mary Alice began to comprehend that her likelihood, realistically, of reaching it in a thriving state was vanishingly small. She was an old woman, after all, in her ninth decade, with still Three decades more to see through before she might emerge, a living, independent woman, from the mirror. How long could a person live? She recalled spans of life from the Bible that rendered her an infant by comparison, and so there was hope for her; and yet, this was not a Biblical time, nor environment, and a woman of her years in this world should expect at any moment the swift, grim swish of the scythe and, subsequently, the terror of a senseless infinity. If so: all for nought, her seemingly eternal endurance of this glassy prison ... and there hadn't even been daffodils for years and years. Rowan had never paid her much attention, not like Melissa; but then again, when it Counted, he'd come through, and so she harbored no unkind sentiments in his regard.

Her mirror now her deathbed, did Mary Alice still think of Norbert? Yes! And so fondly... no longer recalling her speculations that her carefree dancing had provoked his vengeance, now she remembered dancing *with* him, his smiling eyes gazing into hers as they circled and swept the chamber—her body limber in his embrace—his posture erect and masculine—her sighs audible, sweet, and tuned to his smooth, baritone humming, which was the music of their promenade.

And they continued to dance. It was all she had left to reflect from her mirror: time itself, composed in steps, her memories. A memory, for example, of a young man, who perhaps had been unduly stern, perhaps intemperate, perhaps... any number of unpleasant adjectives, but who, most critically, had loved her in his own way. And here he was, finally, returned to her so vividly after all these years, and she was not alone anymore—for it really was him—and he was always with her now, Norbert, yes, *Norbert*, that man whose chest received her leaning cheek, that man whose arms held her firmly through the steps, that young man, though not a handsome one, *per se*, yet beautiful for being so young, and loving her so terribly that he had put her in a mirror rather than share her with the world... and she (had she ever been otherwise?) young... joined by Norbert, he, too, still young... yes, now both of them eternally their most vigorous and vital versions in the inviolable stronghold of their mirror, dancing for years in a dusty room at the end of the hall as they waited patiently together for their freedom to arrive... Meanwhile, Rowan's mother passed, Rowan and Melanie juggled responsibilities, Patty pubesced, visitors visited, deliverymen delivered, and the house remained always the cynosure of a vast rotation that was the life and love of a family in the world.

Although she was entirely unaware of the history surrounding it, Patty did occasionally visit the mirror room, and even found a strange note once, which she tore from the notebook and brought to her own room for study:

It seems Our Lady's life was not long enough to gain her freedom. Your kind efforts were not wasted, however; she was given hope to last her through the time—as was I—and that is no small thing.

I trust you do not mind: I have joined my Mary Alice in the mirror. She sends her love and wishes to remind you: Please try to keep things tidy, and do bring back the daffodils.

—Norbert

The girl puzzled over these words for a few minutes before slipping the paper between the leaves of her *Visual Encyclopedia of the Human Anatomy*, after which she quite forgot about it (her habit of mind more musical than visual). A few years later, her mother Melanie packed the book, among others, in a box labeled "Give."

ROCKING HORSE TRAFFIC

I awoke from my usual dream (rocking horse traffic) to find my father's hands fiddling inside my stomach.

"Just making an adjustment," he assured me, but I felt uneasy all the same. I had been aware of nothing amiss, nothing needing adjustment... and usually, my father informed me in advance of these operations.

My head sought comfort from my fluffy pillow, and I submitted to his ministrations placidly. I was accustomed to this pain... I "stepped aside" and revived highlights of my dream to pass the time. The horses' eyes were black, and their teeth were white, or possibly the reverse.

After a few minutes, my father carefully sewed my belly up and said, "Okay, good morning, Bobby!"

Grinning, his forelock wayward, he bent to kiss my brow; the pleasant, foamy mist of his breath diffused over my face and warmed me back into my body.

"Hungry for breakfast?"

I wasn't hungry, but I nodded, my assent habitual to my father's queries. It's not that I don't dare to disagree with him, but only that I can't see why I should.

My somber mien, perhaps, elicited a smile from my father, and he ruffled my hair. I always giggle when he does this—it is one of our rituals of affection—but this time, I failed.

Instead, I coughed and felt some wetness on my lower lip.

My father, squinting at me, frowned and said, "Shit." He wiped my mouth with his smooth finger, and I glimpsed the familiar dark goo of my blood upon its tip as he hastily withdrew it.

"Well," he said, rubbing the finger clean on his cotton smock, "Well... hum... After breakfast, Bobby. Just a little adjustment, that's all. We'll have you fixed up, let's just see what breakfast does, okay?"

I made to gather my strength to heave myself from bed, but my father scooped me up and carried me into the kitchen in the baby way. I enjoyed the ride, feeling weightless yet secure pressed up against his manly chest, although the faint, coppery scent of my bloodstain on his smock instilled me with a touch of nausea.

I had been doing well the last week or so. My limbs had been strengthening, my muscles building and stretching, my lungs swelling to a new capacity. I had played on the playground... the slide, the swings, even the merry-go-round... I had "frolicked," as my father bade me do, my breath become an exhilarating wind streaming through me, my body a trumpet blown triumphantly.

This morning, however, I felt strange again, and weak... listless... like before. I considered revealing these symptoms to my father, but I didn't want to disappoint him.

It's okay, I thought, *we'll wait to see what breakfast does.*

My father sprinkled walnuts and raisins on my cereal. I don't like them, but I didn't protest. I was hardly strong enough to lift the spoon up to my mouth, or even to grind the food between my molars.

He sat across the table, watching me eat. I pointed with my spoon to his barren placemat, and he waved his hand dismissively. "I already had mine," he said, but I knew that was not true. He always brushed his teeth after a meal, yet there had been no spearmint on his breath.

My bowl emptied only by half, I set my spoon down and hung my head. My father came around and knelt by my chair. His arms wrapped around me and drew me close. His cheek and nose were cool in my neck.

"It's okay, just eat what you can."

His voice's thrum became my flesh.

"I love you, Bobby."

My seam throbbed.

"Let's see what we've got, huh?"

He lifted me up and took me into the bathroom, setting me on my feet in front of the toilet. I steeled myself not to "step aside" this time: I couldn't poop without my spirit.

Afraid to split my belly's fresh stitches by bending, I made magic motions with my hands that compelled my father to pull down my pajamas for me. Upon exposure, my pecker immediately squirted a limpid stream onto his smock. I backed myself onto the toilet-seat and began to cry.

My father made a cooing noise deep in his chest, his customary mode of consolation, and he ruffled my hair, but my crying increased. Weakness flurried down my ribs in nauseating waves. Something was strange and wrong inside of me.

"Just give it a shot," he murmured.

I gave it a shot—filling my lungs, straightening my spine, and contracting all my muscles in the way my father'd taught me. As I strained, a blade of pain sliced rhythmically down my torso, whimsically hacking at my organs. I could not sustain the effort, and I relaxed, leaning back against the tank as I gasped for breath.

"Anything?" my father asked, peering avidly between my legs. I spread them apart to improve his view, but I knew, without looking, that the water would be clear.

My father emitted a frustrated sigh. "What, what... maybe the kefir? Let's try that, what do you think?"

I found myself too weak to respond in any manner, save a few blinks. My father kissed the top of my head and said, "I'll be right back, Bobby. I've got the flavored kind, you'll love it."

When my father was gone, my mother "stepped in." Her eyes were round, as though frightened, but that was just an illusion stemming from the spiritual effect: her smile, genuine, was radiant with her love, and she waved to me.

I could not wave back; I could not move.

Her smile increased—she was always keen to encounter me when I could not afford resistance—and she reached for my hands, commenced to guide them toward my belly. I tried to shake my head and to pull my arms away, but in my weakened condition, no movements were possible for me, other than those my mother directed.

I could not "step aside," since my mother's grasp was immitigable, and so, for the moment, I had to endure the agony. My mother used my fingernails to slice the criss-cross threads and speared my fingers deep into the peeling seam... establishing a grip upon the flaps... followed by a heaving wrench that opened me up... and out spilled my slimy tubes, unfurling everywhere—draped across my legs, piled up on the floor, and even slithering down between my thighs to fill the toilet-bowl.

Once she was satisfied that I was inside-out and dead, my mother released her grip so that she could grab for my second body, the one I employed to "step aside"... as ever, she wanted me to "step out," in order to be with her, but I am an agile boy in some respects: I "stepped aside" just in time, away from her reach, and I found myself among the horses.

Far away, I could hear my mother scream her rage and sorrow. As her long shrieks faded, I began also to hear my father's wails. Unable to resist my curiosity, I peeked.

In the bathtub lay a discarded bottle of kefir, its maroon and viscous contents—a raspberry flavor, perhaps, which I'm sure I would have enjoyed—glugging languorously out of the neck into a thick, expanding pool.

My father, frantically, was gathering up my numerous and lengthy tubes from the floor and toilet-bowl. His tears splashed all over them as he stuffed them into an oily trash bag.

My mother had fled. She preferred to keep her distance from my father.

With the bag in one hand and my limp body slung over his opposite shoulder, my father hurried out of the bathroom and rushed toward the surgical theater he maintained in the garage. I left him to his duty, trusting him to fix me up—he never failed in this task. Never.

To pass the time, I entertained myself among the horses. Some were on rockers, some sustained on poles, others balanced on their prancing feet. Their jowls were sudsy, but not wet, no... rather, a sculptural froth.

Indeed, everything about them was sculptural... the wind-shaped manes, the bulging, frenzied eyes, the realistic sweat drops on their muscular haunches... and painted... so many variant hues, yet combined without discord... without exception, these mystical colors glowing outward in accordance with a harmonious principle.

A silence reigned, as was usual in this spiritual world. But no, a susurration seemed manifest, a gentle rhythm upon my senses... so it was a breathing silence.

I sensed in this "breathing silence" a plenitude of tides and forces... measureless activity... conversations among men and spirits... creatures historical and mythical... material and oneiric... an endless parade of characters and events. The choices so profuse, I could attend to none of them; yet I chided myself for my confusion, my constructed retreat into this typical dream of rocking horse traffic.

It struck me that a particular horse appealed to me more than the others. Unlike them, its eyes were shut, concealing from me the frightening, manic stare that characterized all the sculpted beasts in this region. Its dappled hide was pleasing—brown and white with flecks of redness—and the smooth, worn saddle upon its back invited me to sit there.

I mounted up, and held the reins with a ginger care. I am not practiced in the riding of horses; I had never dared before to stride one, only to wander among them and occasionally stroke their hard, cool skin. Not knowing what else to do, I commenced to rocking... and the silence of the world scampered into hiding... chased away by the slow creak of my steed's rockers.

As if powered by the energy of my "trot," the world around me began to roll by. What before had been a blank screen transformed into a movie.

Stars blinkered in and wheeled about on multiple axes. Continents floated on oceans of liquified rock. I saw multitudes of people swarming on the landscapes, and within their brains were other swarms, and within their bodies infestations... scarabs scuttling through the pipes... spiders with a hundred eyes, all useless in the dark... and babies, so many human babies, defective in their manufacture, curled into balls and ready for disposal. And so much more—all possible forms of disease, invasion, squalor, and somatic decrepitude.

Then, the movie settled into a story, for which the preceding montage had merely served as prelude.

I saw a surgical theater, the very one in my father's garage. I saw my father and my mother, both embodied, both alive... my mother alive... embodied... the idea had never occurred to me.

My living mother was laid out on the table—so familiar to me from my own numerous operations and adjustments— her limbs strapped down, her chest sawn open and, within that cavity, her lumpen heart exposed and quivering with its living pulses.

My father bent over her, performing adjustments in the meat with gleamy instruments, his concentration as intense as I had ever seen it. My mother was asleep, and yet soon evoked to wakefulness by the sound of a weakly keening voice—my own voice, I realized.

My keening voice, but not mine, no... a baby's voice.

I spurred my rocking horse beyond its creaking gait, impelled it to a gallop's pace, and the film sped up commensurately.

My mother's head ratcheted from side to side, her eyeballs spinning frantically, searching for the source of her child's cries. I saw, from my vantage, that the baby mewled in its playpen... my playpen... my... my cries incited by a ragged suture in my neck that had been torn by contact with an exposed velcro strap in the playpen's netted siding.

My mother could not locate me. From my present saddle, I attempted to speak to her, to inform her, but I could not speak, not in this... body.

Not from this mount, not from this dream, not from this

time.

What I saw could not be altered; it was a scene drawn from the world's memory, a fixed image, upon which I could only gaze and seek to store it in my own memory.

My revery had slowed me near to stillness, and the actors on the screen now moved with excruciating care as in a cinematic scene of slow-motion catastrophe.

My father set his hand upon my mother's shoulder to steady her. "Liiinnnnddddaaa," he said, "Caaaalllmmmm yooourrrrsssseeeeeellfff."

I spurred my steed into a canter. I yearned for speed, but also wished for time to observe the details.

My father strapped my mother's head to still her struggles, and he caressed the perspiration from her brow and cheeks. "It's okay, honey," he said, infusing his voice with cheer, although his expression was worried and ghastly with exhaustion. "Bobby's just had a little accident. I'll have him fixed up in a jiffy, and then we'll put the finishings on your repairs. Shouldn't be much longer."

He limped over to the playpen and lifted out the baby, a soothing lullaby humming from his chest. Gently, he placed me on the changing table and began to inspect the damaged stitch.

Meanwhile, my mother's fingers curled inward and prodded at the strap that bound her wrist. Slowly, carefully, she managed to loosen the velcro's grip until her wrist was freed. Then she freed her head and her other limbs.

When she stood up, her heart slipped out of its station and dangled down her sternum. Although she tried, she could not stifle her agony's croak. My father turned and cried out.

"No, Linda! Get back on there!"

My mother cradled her heart in her hands and swayed. Her voice a hoarse whisper, she said, "It's all a shambles, John, it's no good."

My father shook his head placatingly, but his eyes betrayed a desperate sheen. "Lie back down, it'll be all right, I swear." He lifted up the baby and made to return me to the playpen. "Just lie down, honey, and I'll have that fixed up in time for dinner. You know me."

"I do, I do, John, and I love you, and I love Bobby, too." With that, her jaw opened wide, and she took a bite from what she held.

Before he could reach her, she had already chewed and swallowed half the muscle. Wailing, my father tried to fix it up, but he simply didn't have the materials.

I awoke from this dream to find myself upon the operating table. My father leaned over me, his smile resurgent and relieved.

"All better now, Bobby, that was a close call."

I peered down and saw that my belly was sewn back up. I tensed my muscles, attempting to sense the presence of my organs, and a small, gray loop of intestine poked out between two sutures.

My father flinched and said, "Oops. Hum, well, that's not a problem." He took up his scalpel and flicked at the surrounding stitches, then pried apart the flaps to gain access to the errant organ.

I opened and shut my mouth a few times for practice, licked my lips, and said, "Daddy." My throat burned with the unaccustomed speech, and my father paused his work to look at me, amazed.

"Yes... Bobby?"

"What happened to my mother?"

He scowled and shook his head with annoyance, but then his features assumed a more sorrowful shape, and he sighed. "No point dwelling there, Bobby. No point at all." His eyes met mine and softened, then shifted away again. "There's nothing... can't be fixed."

"Daddy," I whispered. "I love you, Daddy."

My father looked surprised and grateful, even jubilant—then suddenly bewildered as I took the scalpel from his unwary fingers and drew it across his throat. His hot blood rained upon me, soon filling all the spaces in my opened belly, and we both relaxed into a torporous pose.

Together, then, at long last and hand-in-hand, we "stepped out" to join you, Mother.

THE LIFE OF CHERRY

No one possesses himself! Detestable thought! No one possesses himself! Thus everything belongs to the others! Don't we own even our faces? Do they belong to anybody who chooses to look at them? And one's body? Can others own one's body?

—Pär Lagerkvist, *The Dwarf*

TABLE OF CONTENTS

A MAIDEN'S PORTION

ALONE IN THE WORLD

You are alone in the world, said the penis to the cervix. Your exit is blockaded, and only I may penetrate your isolation.

The cervix bowed her head, smiling to herself. She knew better—the penis was here for shore leave, solely, and soon enough would decamp to other ports, leaving her free to entertain a host of foreign sailors from oh so many exotic and cultural locales!—but she did crave, at that instant, the proffered relief, and issued a brazen, come-hither titter before replying with a more becoming modesty, I am conquered! I seek no exit! Do whatever you want!

Whereupon, the penile boat disboarded. Among those hordes that pillaged and pioneered unto the deep of a Dark Continent, a quixotic hero on his own divinely instilled mission charged a windmill that turned out to be the boudoir conversion of a plucky, if bohemian, native maiden, who, charmed by his eccentric approach, permitted him alone into her lace-strewn miracle and swooshed shut the door behind them.

The hero and the maiden joined in revelry and soon forgot themselves... and in their joining and forgetting multiplied into a protoplasmic joy of terrifying scale that soon dwarfed the very landscape and installed itself into the firmament as a glittering galaxy that stretched across every angle of the view... and so began the life of Cherry.

Swelling and swirling in the maternal empyrean, Cherie, whose toddler lips one day would plump her name into the fruit that would become her namesake, experienced a rhapsodic comfort and thus developed a predisposition to dreaminess that would sketch the contours of her character for years to come.

Her mother loved her, yet brutally discharged her from the murmuring darkness of her pleasant eternity into a babble of beeps and radiant bulbs, forcing her ears and eyes to ingest too soon the gruel and grog of sensual stimulation.

She was now a body, not a celestium...

... her name Cherie, soon enough Cherry...

... and how difficult, how unexpected and unplanned for, this unrequested transition from one state to its opposite...

The world did nothing to ease the abrupt pain of her making, rather assaulted her pitilessly with a continuous sensation, in her now too solid heart, of me and mine and I-am-what. This sensation would never cease throughout the life of Cherry, regardless of her provisional name or whether tears blotted her sight behind their jellied scrim or keening scissored through the volutional ramparts of her ears.

We cannot deny that from one end of her life to the other, Cherry was a body most reliably, and a spirit in but fits and starts. From time to time, she thought she ranged abroad into the ecstasy of being other than herself... but inside of her, always, the heart hugged its own meat again and again and again, a squeeze and a smooch and a pause for vibrato with a drunken hiccough, triumphantly and everlastingly repeated for every corresponding second of the life of Cherry.

There was no quiet in the crib, no, no substitute found in there for the womb's engulfment. Cherie mewled without relent, and in shuffled Mother, occasionally Father, to rearrange the swaddle or set the angel bears, those high flyers, into tinkly swoops across the infant's sky.

Only sleep redressed the crime of her existence, reproducing the sensorium—so recently relinquished—of eternity's love; often, indeed, she retreated into that dark nostalgia, so much more soothing to an infant's brays than the alternative sensorium of piss, shit, and angel bears that was her crib... and invading from an adjacent room, muffled by a wall with blankie hangings and a quilted door an inch ajar, raging voices battering against each other while the furniture turned over with passionate clunks and crashes to satisfy the world's requirement for harmony between the psychical and the physical.

Cherry, a number of years later, on the eve of her death—unprompted and to no attendants—muttered the word she'd heard so often in her crib, before the syllables were more than brute sensation to her brain... and still she did not understand it: yousickpervertedfuck.

She did not distinguish, in those earliest months beyond the womb but prior to her personality, between the instrument of her body and the music produced from it by the world's innumerable fingers. Her sensual receptors were of one piece with the stimulations that played upon them; indeed, the receptors themselves—eyes, ears, mouth, skin—were nearly invisible to her and seemed simply to constitute a wall bounding what existed from what did not.

Thus, what existed: bright, loud, sweet, press.

What did not: me, mine, I-am-what.

Of course, those things did exist and patiently awaited her acknowledgement; indeed, they tortured her with their insistence on her consciousness. Her heart, though tiny, was relentless in its driving rhythm, banging ceaselessly behind the wall of her perceptions...

… it was only a matter of time before she noticed—amidst the clash and clamor of the world's excitements—a beautiful, percussive music emanating from a hidden chamber…

… and instantly upon perceiving it, she would recognize that she was that abiding rhythm, and the rhythm was her: the sensoria, after all, were only entertainment.

In her automated cradle, Cherie babbled to the angel bears and rolled from side to side, her movements synchronized with her heart's metronome, and also syncopated intricately, subtly, with the mechanized rhythm of the rocking crib.

As the hot wax of her prenatal eyes hardened in the cool postnatal air, her vision clarified, and the ursine æronauts who were her most devout attendants assumed a sharp, profound significance. Among all the visual stimulations of the world, theirs was the most lifelike, the most comforting to a lone baby.

The ecstasy of fur and flight. Union of the eye with all that it beholds. To rise along a bear's gaze, to spin in place until the self is viewed from a high redoubt, to be all the bears at once and the baby below, all simultaneously and with certainty.

This is the spirit form.

And yet—insistent—raucous but rhythmic—again and again—the heart hugs to itself… the meat so well-loved, the music driven and percussive, a rich and dense sensorium overwhelming all others, an exclusive preserve in the body brooking no alternatives.

Wrath shimmering in the world's walls and furniture thundering upon the floors and angels tinkling from the sky… all was squeezed and its juice absorbed into the meat of Cherry's heart—a nutritious slurry of me and mine and I-am-what—a slow enrichment of the blood as new, thin humours thickened to vitality with the unconditional love of raging voices.

MOTHER'S PATCH

The spirit form does not preserve or even touch its corresponding body.

Cherie learned this truth merely months, not even a year, into her life. Being among the bears, dangling with them from the firmament, harmonizing with their tinkle choirs, gazing upon all stimulations with equanimity through pitch-clouded vitric orbs: her spirit form, by fiat, was abandoned between one second and its successor, or rather, one might say, its bonds were loosened. The angel bear that she had been continued to fly through the Universe, without Cherie but sometimes nearby. (This bear never learned of Cherry, knew only Cherie, and so Cherie's name remained consistent from birth onward, at the very least, in the world's unseen yet possibly more precious precincts.)

What fiat? The only one that matters to a body.

Pain—instantaneous—arbitrary...

... searing agony delivered by Mother, alongside a soothing voice, shushing, loving, calm with madness...

... Father banging on a locked and blockaded door, barreling his failure into it, voice raging, helpless, high, and sweet...

... and a monstrous voice—Cherie's—shrill—continuous—everlasting—its notes echoing down the remaining corridor of the life of Cherry.

The patch was effected with a swatch of skin from Mother's thigh and a flatiron that had been heated for an hour on the stove's rear burner...

... Cherie's maidenhood preserved for life...

... the entrance to it curtained by Mother's own flesh and

cauterized by glowing metal.

That new, flat delta between her thighs, on healing, presented smooth, dark, uncut skin—its only blemish a faint vertical shadow of the mouth that had been silenced.

Mother crowed through the bequilted door and through its ironing board barricade, Yousickpervertedfuck, tryit! Ain'tnothingtherenow! Justtryit!

Back through the door, a response fluttered, muffled by that intervening matter, transformed from words to music, the bassline of masculinity that was Father's pleading voice: Mmm ohm mm ek ga! Ohm boo mmm hewn!

Within the heart of Cherie—Cherry consistently from here on out to reduce confusion and with respect to the noble spirit now flying guilelessly through the Universe—within that organic metronome that syncopated the beat of her parents' roundelay, a deep, self-preserving love was born: a longing for the world's pain to match her own and a cognate lust for the pain itself.

KING DUST

Cherry's scampering feet were never stilled in those early years, not by Mother's screams to Holditdown nor by the whisper of her own mind to Fly off from the ground. Indeed, the constant whirling motion of her feet could be viewed as the revving of an engine that might accomplish what her winglessness precluded: takeoff, soaring freedom, exhilaration, reunion with the spirit form.

Floorboards giggled and coughed from her relentless tickle, and the ceiling condescended to smile at her antics. These were the only amused persons in her orbit.

From her kidneys, canals were dug to replace the useless channels that now led to a smooth, impermeable barricade. These canals wended through treacherous terrain and cascaded into a nearby grotto where the pungent waters were absorbed into abandoned mounds of sod and soil. Only at the saturation point would this mulch sluice away to a dark destiny of pipes and pressure, never to be seen again. There was always more matter to replenish the supply, however, as Cherry chewed her croutons—allotted one-at-a-time by Mother from a jar above the fridge—and licked dust from the walls to offset the spice.

She abstained from floor-licking, as that was King Dust's terrain. He needed every particle to replenish his body, which was constantly dissolving or dying only to be reconstituted in some other part of the room by the power of his will alone. He allocated to Cherry the wall dust, most graciously, for he recognized and respected the developing girl's physiological needs. He also felt—deep down—hardly admitted it to himself—that one day this luscious girl flesh would belong to him. How union between a being of dust and a being of meat could be effected was none of his concern. He simply desired and plotted, and the years passed.

Cherry gained no mass from her regime of dust and croutons. Three feet tall and 33 pounds she remained, ages three through 13, whereupon the advent of Mistress Molly Cuddle transformed her figure toward the feminine ideal through the radical alteration of her diet.

She first encountered Mistress Molly Cuddle in her dream when she discovered 13 red balloons behind the mop pail in the closet and filled them all with precious gases from her own supply (stored in two blue balloons behind her ribs). Immediately, the red balloons swarmed her through the window and rushed her back inside exactly one floor below.

A voice divine gushed out from a room of vasty cushions and divans on Persian rugs, Oh such a sweetsy child! Welcome to the beef boudoir of Mistress Molly Cuddle! Come here you sweetsy thing!

And Mistress Molly Cuddle opened all her arms, all 26 of them, all her rows of bountiful breasts bound up in lace and silk, a Seductress in the ancient mode...

... but also a Mother and a Wet Nurse, as Cherry discovered snuggling in among the mammaries...

... milk flowing thick with cream through her puckered pooch and down her leathern throat...

... nourishing her famished organelles even beyond the dream state...

... so that on waking she would find herself satisfied and ruddy in her flesh.

Now, whenever pangs of hunger tugged on Cherry's

entrails, she sought her succor in her sleep and scurried in to be with Mistress Molly Cuddle, who always welcomed her in silvery tones of sweet surprise and fed her with an eager fervor from those bounteous tits. Soon the body of Cherry began to plump and grow and glow from deep within by means of luminescent Molly's milk that flowed through every cavern and saturated all the loam of Cherry, from the hot, dense inner core to the loose and crusty topsoil of the upper lip.

Once Cherry's body adjusted to an animalian aliment, Mistress Molly Cuddle weaned her to the dream beef...

... her first taste being the soft heart of a lowing calf, extracted fresh and hot for maximum assimilation...

... consumed in collaboration with the calf himself, who offered his breast to the granite knife proffered forth by Mistress Molly Cuddle and taken up by Cherry to initiate and complete the slaughter in one ecstatic sweeping motion...

... his heart chewed to a smooth jelly and swallowed down a rainbow throat...

... delivered into the series of caverns and grottoes that had been washed by Molly's milk into a shimmery paradise of multi-hued moss meadows and mushroom cap forests.

So—by dream—was Cherry's heart supplied with the constituents it needed to increase its right demesne and tune its felt emanations. And soon enough her kidneys, liver, lungs, and brain all too received their beef allotments. We must report, however, that the smooth, insensate patch of skin between her legs, being of her Mother's flesh and not her own, was unreceptive to all beef colonizations... the only failure of Mistress Molly Cuddle's scheme to make a woman of the girl through high nutrition in the dream state.

Beef-encouraged, Cherry's tits emerged from hiding,

whereupon they perched earnestly atop her rib ladder, devout in their vigil for any sign of lips in need of nipples. Families of fur settled in the valleys of her armpits, and shrubbery grew with wild abandon just beyond the borderline of Mother's patch.

Household crouton consumption plummeted, alerting Mother to a serious situation underfoot, or more precisely, no longer underfoot, as Cherry's height had nearly doubled. Mother—taking note of all the new formations of her daughter's body, so perfect now in shape and mass, her anomalous anatomies well beyond the body-building competence of croutons—perceived evidence of good health stolen from her cupboards that she slaved to fill and informed our heroine, Youthiefyouwhoregetout!

Cherry, never having worn a garment, nor even having stepped outside the walls of the apartment (except in dream), could not at first fathom how to comply with Mother's dictum... but she was eager to learn! Beef-emboldened, her body yearned for strangers to brush by on their way to destinations, gazes to exfoliate her flesh with bristles of desire, poets to decrypt all the codes of beauty up and down the length of her.

And so, dressed between two carpet squares fastened by mop strings and safety pins, Cherry rode her new, extravagant rolling hips out of Mother's rooms and into the traffic of the world beyond to begin a grand adventure.

King Dust, among his many other duties, resolved to keep tabs on her trajectory. The body of Cherry was a precious item and must not be relinquished from the precincts of desire.

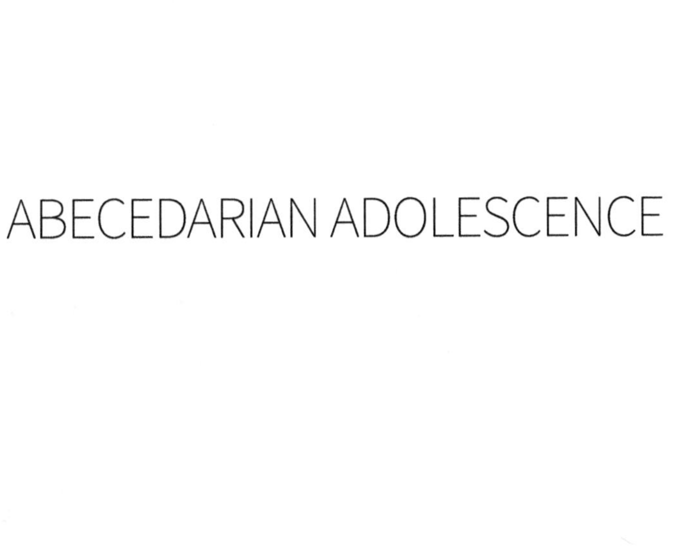

ABECEDARIAN ADOLESCENCE

THE GAZE OF MEN

The gaze of men mercilessly riveted to Cherry's beef-borne beauty, clothed so minimally as she was. She stood upon the pavement pondering the points—north? south? east? west?—for less than one minute before Anatole Beaulieu appeared, mustachioed and monocled, his well-bred voice a model of propriety: I must say, your appearance screams for my attendance, dearie. Utterly screams! So dazed, so childlike! Let me take you home and dress you in all the very pretty frills and flounces that will complement your... your virginal virtues. It would be my special honor!

Her social life heretofore confined to scamperings under Mother's feet and cowerings under Mother's rage with occasional baskings under Mother's unwonted midnight affections—Father's presence mostly mitigated by walls and doors—to be addressed directly in the flesh (not in dream) by a stranger, moreover a male one, overwhelmed our favorite heroine's senses. The pressure of his eyebeam on every stretch of skin it glided o'er, the subtle webbing of his pungent breath about her face, the judgments she inferred from the haste and prickly manners of the passersby, even the trickly vapors gassing off his coat,—all induced in her a tremulous acquiescence to his will, so that she followed him without a peep of protest, eyes cast down and flames of expectation dancing across her shoulderblades.

Undressing Cherry of her trés unsightly carpet remnants was the first order of Anatole Beaulieu's business, which he asserted in a low and lispy faux-chiding voice that hovered close, hot, and damp, a slow current from neck to ear evanescing to a cool mist when he moved away to toss her carpets in the corner.

His second order of business was to gather garments suitable for this wisp of trembling anatomy that vivified his parlor. She was no ordinary girl! Assembled from divine materials! He could see that clearly, even unaware of the dream beef. He begged for inspiration from his prolific cupboards, which generously bestowed a diaphonous lace-trimmed camisole of ballet slipper silk with matching French knickers. The items held her flesh in a cool, voluptuous caress, and Cherry caught a turbulent self-glimpse in the swinging armoire mirror.

But only that glimpse, as the window behind her shattered and the massive figure of Sir Codswallop Dresden—who had observed and then pursued the pair discreetly from the site of their transaction—rampaged in, sweeping Cherry under one arm and with his wolf's head cane driving Anatole Beaulieu under the dresser, where the dandy quivered and wept his loss for the rest of the frog-croaked night.

As Sir Codswallop Dresden beheld the body of Cherry at close quarters, he understood that he would be the sole member of his generation to witness beauty in the carnal format, for the reason that he would possess its only avatar and never share her with another man. Until this moment, Sir Cod had fashioned himself a man of the world, lacking nonsense yet also full of every necessary bit of dander called for by whatever circumstance obtruded... and yet laid low by a nereid! barely budded! not even one ounce of womanly wile in evidence... Very well, so be it, he declared, for every man inevitably arrives unto that stage in his life upon which he must surrender to the vixen Innocence on pain of soul-torture.

Without delay, ensconced in his headquarters, Sir Cod

proceeded to inspect his prize inch by inch, noting the body's exquisite balance of mass and volume mediated by a minimal yet sufficient somatic terrain—geography sublimed to topology. He thought he had transcended our own world to a heavenly estate until he settled down upon the landing pad and discovered entry barred to visitors. Mother's patch was firm in its refusal, and Sir Cod rose up with an ancient anguish. There was another gate, of course, but that one was reserved for barbarians and bimbos, to be eschewed by æsthetes seeking elevation to diviner status... a thought which led to the insight that as the pages of a book must be cut before one reads, so must the sacred book of beauty suffer on the blade of its beholder before relinquishing those precious mysteries so tightly held within.

The Sicilian Edge, his thinnest ceremonial dagger, would suit the task perfectly, and so he laid Cherry tenderly upon his King-Size Water Mattress and went to retrieve that blade from the underground lair of his extensive collection. Much to his chagrin, a lethal spider materialized from the dust around the case that housed the Sicilian Edge and bit Sir Cod decisively dead.

Cherry floated upon the Water Mattress into a gentle dream, in which a mist buoyed her to an island with a cliff and a ranch and a shipwrecked sailor, who saw her with an eyebeam that had not frisked female flesh in more than 60 years of wishing. Ernesto Fortunato swelled with delight at the sudden turn of his luck, only to shrink back into his customary despair discovering Mother's patch, Cherry's permanent decoration in both waking and dream life.

Ernesto was an affable fellow, however, and sustained Cherry with beef from his ranch, demanding only in return her permission for his eyes to rove her body freely, a reasonable exchange in the interest of survival. He also instructed her in every field of knowledge. For the vision of her spongy aureoles he gave her Navigation; for the tight cleft of her buttocks Attic Greek. Astronomy was the prize for her high cheekbones, and the wide parabola of her inner thighs won her all of Analytic Geometry. Every subject was explored until her education was complete, or rather, Ernesto's store of knowledge was exhausted.

After many years, Ernesto Fortunato expired a decrepit but contented man, while Cherry had not aged a day. She woke refreshed and calm, alone in her chamber, and made waves for pleasure on her Water Mattress. As Sir Cod had declined life in answer to a spider's venom, the principle of Adverse Possession assigned his full estate now to Cherry, according to the Common Law Ernesto had bequeathed her in exchange for her perineum.

THE ASCENT OF LADY CHERRY

Lady Cherry surveyed her sudden holdings to establish firmly what belonged to her and what belonged to the world beyond. From a penniless girl with not even clothes to call her own, she had transformed into the Mistress of a mickle estate! Her new purview encompassed tracts of land, bundles of securities, and warehouses of Art, as well as management of menageries, bordellos, office parks, and shopping malls.

Her Certified Agent, George Herrmeister administered her assets with a canny comprehension of what was needed to align her cravings with the world's corruption. She made clear to him her desire for suffering to consume the Universe in a transformative fire, and he clucked sympathetically, naming his fee and securing her signature upon the necessary documents. Since her penmanship had been trained in dream (in exchange for her jawline), she drew her name in the shape of a bear standing on a scaffold, which sufficed for legal purposes.

Mr. Herrmeister first provided Lady Cherry with an inventory of her worldly possessions, enabling her to determine the precise ratio between hers and not-hers. With that proportion established, she merely needed to increase it until all things were contained in her sensorium, merging pain with its infliction, rendering her power absolute over everything that suffered and made others to do so. She had never heretofore understood herself to possess an ambition, but now that she was so well-funded, it seemed to possess her.

Her Agent's next task was to assemble a team of professionals. Executives of the enterprise. Lady Cherry looked with particular favor on the female ones. For example, Inamorata

Jute, CEO of the Whore Division, whose organization was endowed with a mission to gather the seed of men. Vats were installed in the basements of her bordellos, with pipes attached and routed to each whorechamber, where discreet deposition fixtures were fitted with sensors to gauge collection volume and notify a supervisor of any decline in productivity. The vats were periodically emptied into tank cars stamped with the Lady Cherry Logo, her precious payload thus hauled by train to temperature-controlled storage facilities, known as Jute Junctions, that were maintained underground in every major city.

Meanwhile, Lady Cherry instructed Mr. Herrmeister to establish an Institute of Oneiric Learning that would propagate dream pedagogy to the masses. He recruited the eminent and controversial dream seismologist Dr. Kumari Lala to be the Director of Studies. An innovative yet rigorously formal system of instruction that required its pupils only to sleep, the Dream Method swiftly attracted an ardent and even militant movement of advocates devoted to the visionary mission of replacing every school desk with a mattress and every binder with a pillow. There was no limit to class size or participation; entire gymnasia and auditoria were filled with snoozing children of all ages monitored by Dr. Lala's sleep sensors.

The third prong of Lady Cherry's Master Plan was inaugurated when Mr. Herrmeister lured the brilliant renegade economist Mondragon von Newmann into a scheme to establish theoretical foundations for a new system of monetary exchange that would take place exclusively in the dream theater. Dr. von Newmann's research uncovered a vast trove of Menstrual Gold raining eternally from the skirts of Madre Montaña, a mountainous cloud known to hover mostly far out over the molten ocean of humanity's striving, but which occasionally drifted briefly inland, whipping up metallic storms along the coast and raining its treasure upon the rocky beaches of Hope and Honesty. Should humanity gather and store that Menstrual Gold rather than allow it to be reclaimed by the waves, it could serve as a uniquely robust and universal instrument of valuation. With assiduous oversight by a governing body, an abundant supply could be maintained while capping inflation to reasonable levels.

It did not take long for the new system of exchange to take hold in the imagination of the public, for what could be more limpid and liquid than longing? Each person was assigned two tidal pools, one in Hope and one in Honesty. A tidal pool constituted a unique and sedulously maintained Akashic blockchain, recorded in the ætheric fabric of existence itself and counterfeit-proof. A customer, observing an objet du désir, merely had to synthesize enough Menstrual Gold from the purity of his yearning to satisfy the price set by the shopkeeper: Madre Montaña would mediate the transaction by absorbing the specified amount (plus a nominal administrative fee) from his pool of Hope and simultaneously raining it down upon the shopkeeper's puddle of Honesty.

As tidal pools topped up with Menstrual deposits, Lady Cherry's network of companies and organizations mounted a rapid buildout of key hermetic infrastructure—in particular, a fleet of zeppelin cropdusters, the subject of avid gossip among the dream acolytes for months—intended to commingle more intimately than ever before the dreamer with the dreamed. Most crucially, yet overlooked by most, Oneiric Pipe was installed at every Jute Junction, one end fitted to the primary seed vat, the other end to the immense tankcar of a zeppelin cropduster.

Miss Quincy Rabbler, Director of Social and Swapnic Media at Lady Cherry Industries, kicked off a public health campaign promoting the 24-hour Sleep Protocol, a proven anti-aging practice and healthy alternative to a stressful life-style. The effort proved successful, and Lady Cherry estab-lished enormous Sleep Centers in all world capitals to house and maintain a vast army of Protocol adherents. So much dreaming on a planetary scale amplified humanity's ætheric wattage beyond the threshold required to fulfill Lady Cher-ry's design.

Thus did her Master Plan finally come together. Unbe-knownst to the world's economists, even to the brilliant Mon-dragon von Newmann whose esoteric inquiries had made her vengeance practicable, the heart of a nugget of Menstrual Gold was an egg manufactured from the dust of desire that suffuses the Universe—fixed and fecundated by one drop of our feisty heroine's blood—but none had actually yet been fertilized since the seed of men exists only in the somatic terrain.

At Lady Cherry's command, however, her armada of zeppelin cropdusters bombarded the beaches of Hope and Honesty with their full loads, and a new chapter in World History was begun.

THE CONQUERING CLUTCH

The world's denizens did not even realize that their dreams were now under Lady Cherry's dispensation, or that the legions of harrowing figures that romped and rampaged through the ruin of their dreamscapes were in fact the children of her fury.

The crops had grown and budded instantaneously...

... even before the zeppelins had reberthed in their earthly docks...

... as time in the dream world passes not between points, but between events.

Her nearly infinite harvest yielded spawn all smooth between the legs like their progenitor. Male from female could not be discerned in their sexless bodies, and so they took on different roles as it pleased them. Given to life by fiat and endowed by their creator with the will to chaos, the children enacted their splenetic birthright upon the entire dreaming planet. All dreamers were unified in terror of the Clutch, as no dream was exempt from the Clutch's intervention.

The brats were relentless in their scissoring and tearing motions as they cut their way from dream to dream. Their raucous howls rattled all locks and barriers; their despairing wails lingered in every lonesome alley, every dodgy nest, every habitable crevice. Even at rest, their molars ground together in a deafening drone that came to pervade the atmosphere of dreaming. Neither peace nor sanctity obtained in the Clutch's channel, only mayhem. The special grace that is conferred upon a dreaming body was dissipated into anxiety and frenzy. Ancient archetypes whose influence had spanned millennia of human consciousness were smashed by the Clutch's roving disco swarms. The madness of the Clutch even pursued dreamers back into the waking world. Some woke to burning bedclothes, others woke in floods that poured in through the windows. Bedmates woke to find themselves both murdering and murdered.

With trivial ease, the Clutch delivered up to Lady Cherry nearly every portion of dreaming existence that she had not already swallowed within her panglobal power network, and she was on schedule soon to achieve Totality, but for the sudden surge of resistance from an unexpected quarter:

Adjunct Professor Salvatore Tower—internationally renowned expert in Ætheric Studies with a specialization in Lucid Æronautics (and yet still untenured to any University, most likely by his own eccentric preference)—had been promenading in the garden all this time, lost in thought, unaware of dream sea-changes. The decorated Theosophical genius had lately been giving all of his sophisticated cogitative facility over to the tricky conundrum of astral flight in gravity wells—an intellectual theater of a far-distant coordinate—and had thus failed to observe the thorough routing of mankind's dream defenses.

Of course, he reasoned—upon taking note of developments—it could not be permitted! There were still Purposes for humanity in the Universe, Higher ones. Perhaps... one day... it all could end, but let that moment not be premature in its arrival.

His first task, after combing down his infamously overeager cowlick, was to determine the director of the attack, as it was yet unclear to whom the Clutch owed its lineage. For that purpose, he hired Una Vulvalacta, Private Third Eye, to employ her supernal talent to its predestinated end, which was—as he clarified to her during their preliminary interview—to assist the preservation of humanity against its subduction under the magmic wrath of a rogue Erinys.

To her professional credit, she did not eject him then and there, but coolly named her price while valiantly resisting the dimples of his charm. When he agreed and signed the proffered contract, she nodded pleasantly and offered her client some oolong tea before commencing to open her Pineal Eye upon the vasty torment of the dream world.

Ms Vulvalacta perceived easily the thick bundles of ætheric cord tethering the members of the Clutch to their malefic progenitor, whom she identified to Prof. Tower as none other than our Lady of Cherry.

I need a location, Ms Vulvalacta, he declared, coordinates on every ætheric axis please, to which she replied, not even my retainer has been met! Fulfill your obligations, and I'll fulfill mine! He did, and she did: the Guest Pavilion of the Baleful Temple in the East of the Sunken Sun. I should have guessed, declared our irrepressible and utterly endearing Adjunct Professor, hot on the heels of his quarry; meanwhile his cowlick sprang adorably amiss.

A jinriksha bustled along a dusking road deep in the Eastern territories; huddled together behind a makeshift canopy for privacy, Prof. Salvatore Tower and his research assistant Willem Xingham discussed in whispers the known details of Lady Cherry's life story. Her roots in benighted obscurity, her unlikely rise to cultural prominence, her shady business deals, and significantly: her strange disappearance from public life at the very moment that the Clutch had commandeered the dreamplane.

Falling into a brown study, the boyish Theosophist murmured gently into his monogrammed hanky: With apologies, dear girl, your tale is deplorably tragic... but we must end this travesty before it ends us.

THE LIFE OF YUMI ZEEMI

THE SINGING DAMSEL

Lady Cherry empowered the Clutch from her redoubt in the Guest Pavilion of the Baleful Temple, which offered maximum comfort and luxury to the woman of means who wished to dream unseen and undisturbed by worldly interference. The compound was nestled in an ærie isolated from all human contact, while an oneiric screen shielded the property from observation in ætheric realms (howbeit, as we've seen, ineffective against pineal eyes). There was no way to approach undetected, and indeed, Prof. Tower and Willem Xingham did not seek to conceal their arrival.

The dream monks of the Baleful Temple mounted a vigorous defense of the sprawling subtile grounds, and their astral acrobatics presented a formidable challenge to Prof. Tower's martial prowesses. Fortunately, Willem's akasic forté was to channel multiple fighting bhutas through his fingertips, thus deviating and blunting the monks' sharp ethereal vectors, which Prof. Tower was then able to dissipate categorically through employment of arcane alchemical methodologies accessible only to the most advanced Theosophical adepts.

Thus admitted to the chambers of the legendary Lady Cherry herself, Prof. Tower beheld the fierce commander of all dream legions currently overrunning the immaterial world, and he was—it cannot be denied—in that very instant—besmitten. Perhaps he may be excused that beauty born of beef cannot be withstood by a mortal man. So well versed in the most esoteric subjects of Theosophy and Alchemy, our Prof. Tower surely possessed the tools to hold fast against mere terrestrial allure, but in her slumbered sprawl—wispily bodied, diaphanously gowned, peaceful and careless as a child even while her dreaming body directed the Eschaton—our darling Cherry proved irresistible!

Compelled to lie down upon her—bodily, yet as in a dream—Prof. Tower became not as himself but as an avatar of an imperturbable Eminence, incapable of doing other than he did now, without consideration or discipline, but with passion and dedication, all his bodies—ætheric, astral, mental, buddhic—unitary in the purpose of achieving the salvation of humanity in a single instant of erumpent play...

... Mother's patch unyielding...

... and yet...

... permeable, perhaps, to a gentle spray of moisture—at a particular temperature—under a particular degree of pressure—in a particular rhythm of application...

... and therefore vulnerable to a rare but occasionally recorded phenomenon in the male somatosphere...

... spontaneous gonadal off-gassing—so rare but also so exquisite of sensation—present only in cases of the most drastic desire fulfillment...

... generating spermatazoic vapors capable of crossing any membrane without hindrance.

In this way, a warm fog suffused the inner chambers of the Lady Cherry, condensing into a glistening coat upon every surface it encountered. Indeed, our eager Theosophite's prolific gonads applied several such coats over the course of his precious hour.

A lovely music sprang up, pervading all the manse of Lady Cherry's womb, and from what source we could not at first discern, until investigation delivered us into a bedchamber gilded all in Menstrual Gold, wherein a damsel lazing cozy 'neath a heavy comforter sang sweet tones that were sonically enhanced by the fresh acoustic paint upon the walls and fixtures. The heightening pleasures of the aural atmosphere beheated and provoked her to throw off her bedclothes, reclining in the nude 'neath the 'nointment of the fog.

The echoing fog absorbed the singing damsel—and she the fog—the two amalgamating for all time into a new living substance that swiftly swelled to occupy every chamber and indeed constructed more when those proved inadequate to contain its wondrous bulk.

And so, within the many-chambered womb of Cherry— where the singing never ceased but rang through the rooms continually clear and sweet—began the life of Yumi Zeemi, named not by Adjunct Professor Salvatore Tower (whom Cherry never met in any body but the physical, and who therefore vanished from our story immediately upon fathering the savior of mankind), nor by Willem Xingham (who had witnessed the holy event described above and, profoundly impressed, went on to found an unprecedented yet successful semiannual glossy publication devoted to Theosophically themed erotica designed to simultaneously enlighten and despoil the consciousness of all beholders), but by Cherry herself.

Cherry's maternity of Yumi Zeemi induced her to revise her Master Plan: no longer to impose an incandescent final justice on a world of cruel misuse, but instead—an option Mother's patch had always seemed implacably to thwart—to love and house a baby in that selfsame world, shielding it from all pain and thereby defeating cruel-intentioned Fate even more decisively than had she conquered and devoured all the dreaming lands.

Lacking Lady Cherry's direction, the Clutch disbanded promptly, its individual members reduced in purpose and intensity. These slackened figures may still be encountered wandering the countrysides—foraging in the brush for insect snacks or playing jacks on pounded dirt well away from the road, skinnydipping in the lily pond, perhaps, or hanging nonchalantly by the knees from thick tree branches—until such time as they are called again to wreak calamity upon an unsuspecting world of dream. Some few members, however—all constrained to the female form—were bound by Mama Cherry as Staff to serve her impending household. These lucky attendants donned starchy garments and prepared her estate to receive its new family.

Yumi Zeemi lacked a traditional path from the fortress of Mama Cherry's womb into the world. Thus by Caesar's method (administered by the Staff surgeon) was her way facilitated, and while Mama Cherry was expecting another patch, somewhat larger than Mother's, to seal the slice, the Staff seamstress essayed instead to suture it with needle and thread, a far more elegant (and reversible) solution to unwanted openings, bethought our heroine.

No beeps nor bulbs greeted young Yumi's grand entrance. Instead: candles, incense burners, melodious tones from the Staff flautist. Upon arrival—right away—Yumi Zeemi began to sing, and did not cease for many years to come.

DREAM AND DIRT

Brought up equally in dream and dirt, Yumi Zeemi made no distinction between the two. Trodding both the ebullient turf of dream meadows and the ancient stolid geologic earth—the way always cleared of dangers by her vigilant Mama—she pliéed, spun, leapt, arched, and somersaulted through her childhood unresisted by any worldly or oneiric impediment.

Mama Cherry enlisted Mistress Molly Cuddle as her wet nurse and weaned the child to the dream beef as soon as her gums were strong enough to mash flesh to a swallowing consistency. Yumi took to beef with the unbridled ecstasy of a human organism that has never known sorrow. Her viscera pranced and played with delight in the Eden of her body, even as her body pranced and played in the Eden of the world her Mama dreamed around her, and her limbs stretched into gracile batons enabling her pirouettes and cartwheels.

And always: singing. The parting of Yumi's lips never failed to loose the sweetest melodies and harmonies ever heard by an exposed ear. The Staff musicologist remained always in earshot, transcribing every note for posterity (while murmuring to herself in ecstasy). Meanwhile, the Staff poet stayed busy composing lyrics euphonious enough to accompany such transportive tones.

No visitors were allowed into the mickle estate of Mama Cherry. Yumi Zeemi was home schooled (with the avid assistance of the Staff tutor, a hard disciplinarian with a heart of Menstrual Gold) in all the subjects her Mama had previously mastered at considerable expense—her sensorium unsullied by the admission of any person not her Mama or her Mama's Staff. Indeed, the steady orbit of the Staff Sun warmed and illuminated an upbringing so intricately designed (and shielded from corrosive external influence) that unyielding happiness was the only possible outcome.

And there was no cease to her singing. Her voice, so naturally mellifluous and melismatic, carried well and thus reverberated perpetually across the campus of Mama Cherry's estate, entwined in every activity: the Staff gardener's shears fell into syncopation with the rhythm of her song; the Staff philosopher inquired into the role of music in formulating consciousness; the Staff cattle hand hummed gentle ditties to her charges, who also lowed in concert with the pervading music; far out in the woods that hemmed in the grounds, warm and content beside her cozy campfire, the Staff hobo hoisted her trusty harmonica to her lips and improvised a serene accompaniment to that dulcet voice drifting in on the evening breeze.

The Staff recruiter, in particular, had big ideas. She used her contacts in the Industry to spread the word about this volcanic talent that was going to inundate the Pop landscape. She enlisted the Staff publicist to hunker down beneath Yumi's bed and whisper all night of the purported delights of fame and universal adoration. What wouldn't a girl give, she asked, to be loved by everyone? And Yumi replied dreamily, I already am loved by everyone. Oh? came the whisper, Everyone in Mama Cherry's yard loves you, that's a fact. But there is a world beyond, did you know, chockablock with people Mama Cherry can not boss around! Who are they? asked Yumi. They are themselves, came the whisper, and that is what makes their love so powerful. They will love you not at your Mama's command, but with their own hearts. Imagine how that must feel!

And she did just that: imagined. How it must feel to be loved not for that you are, but for what you are.

At breakfast, Yumi Zeemi ventured her idea aloud, I want to be a Pop Star!

Mama Cherry smiled indulgently and said, That is a lovely dream, beloved.

Not only in dream, said Yumi. I want my singing to resound throughout the empyrean of human consciousness! To expose and crystallize the longings of all those people in the world beyond! To orient their desire toward me and fixate their happiness upon my being the glitteriest star in their firmament!

Hmm, her Mama Cherry replied.

It seemed possible to fulfill the wish without exposing Yumi Zeemi to the ravages of contact with the human race. Their love would stream in by the special grace of Pop Stardom, but that would be the limit of their contact with her precious daughter, either in body or in spirit. She could achieve the fame she coveted while yet remaining safely sealed within the haven of Mama Cherry's estate.

What will be your stage name? she asked, and Yumi sailed about the room with glee and hovered in a pensive glimmer just below the chandelier, weighing out the possibilities. She swam back down to kiss her Mama on the cheek and clasped her hands together charmingly beneath her chin as she declared, I am Diva Yumi Zeemi!

Without delay, the Staff recruiter signed her to a Major Label and scheduled a series of recording sessions with the Staff producer. Meanwhile, the Staff publicist tirelessly pumped the Buzz, ensuring that Diva Yumi Zeemi was the name in circulation among the au courant tastemakers and cultural curators of the Mode, both high and low. Thus, a brilliant (howbeit brief) career began.

A FRIENDSHIP FOR THE AGES

Diva Yumi Zeemi had a secret: she embedded within every song she released a miniaturized simulacrum of Diva Yumi Zeemi. Her spy was so tiny that no one—not even Mama Cherry—ever noticed it tucked between the sound waves.

As a song traveled through the worlds, entering ears for direct admission into the minds and hearts of her fans, it deposited its stowaway deep within. Taking up permanent residence, unnoticed by its host, her spy reported back to her continually what it saw and felt in every territory. By this means, she knew everything about her fans—all of them—and she loved them all equally and passionately.

Was it even possible to love one fan more than all the others? Even, perhaps, to love one in exclusion of all the others? To renounce Pop Stardom and transform into a humble, faithful fan of someone else?

We found our answers on a fencepost. Lazing there, waiting for a squirrel or other unsuspecting morsel to scamper by, a cat named Monsieur Mew perked his ears to imbibe of the exquisite melody trickling down from the nearby window, upon whose sill was perched a transistor radio tuned to a distant AM station. Ommm, he sensually purred...

... stretching his bulk in preparation for a venturing forth and an investigation...

... yet he needed not to venture anywhere to glean a response to his feline curiosity...

... for Diva Yumi Zeemi's spy entered boldly, making no attempt to conceal her infiltration, assuming herself invisible...

... however, M. Mew being a cat, and thus inquisitive of every visitor in every register of scale—whether person-sized or pixie-sized—inquired of her right away...

... and a friendship for the ages thus began:

Who are you? asked M. Mew of the girlish singer in his head, who dutifully relayed his query to her Diva.

Surprised and delighted to be so addressed (and by such an unusual fan), her Diva replied—and she faithfully conveyed—I am Yumi Zeemi.

Ommm, purred M. Mew, No, darling, I am me & can't see you.

To which she giggled.

He continued, Unless... Are you me? (More giggles.) You are... my you? (Guffaws.) Perhaps, you are my you, me! (Gales.)

Through her shrieks: No, silly! I am Yumi!

I prefer... My Yumi. Please be mine, you seem so yummy. (Gleeful cackles.)

And so on and so forth. How insinuating a cat may be! How seductive! See him curl his tail in...

... now see him twitch and switch it! How he turns his gaze elsewhere...

... while yet maintaining his regard...

... so sly, so cunning...

... so self-attentive and yet generous...

How long was it before M. Mew had persuaded Diva Yumi Zeemi to elope with him into the Cat Cosmos, an untraceable parallel Creation where they could bask together in euphoric intimacy, well away from the cloistered tyranny of Mama Cherry's love?

Not long!

There are things I need to do, explained M. Mew—in skillful culmination of his whirlwind courtship of the girlish wonder in his head—things I simply can not do without my Yumi. (No more giggles now, only solemn, silent preparations. She was not a singer anymore.)

So did Diva Yumi Zeemi relinquish her iconic rôle and exalted cultural status—as well as her inheritance—to elope with M. Mew...

... to commit her living energy to the fulfillment of his projects...

... cherishing him and being cherished...

... in another story altogether.

And so did Mama Cherry—subsequently failing to locate her Yumi in any world of dream or dirt—commence her crumble.

ADVERSE POSSESSION

ALONE IN THE WORLD

Cherry would not stay at her estate—now all silent as if no singing ever had suffused it—the Staff stricken, the mansion morose, the parlor petulant—and so she packed a bindle and lighted out to visit the only person she thought might solve her desolation.

You sweetsy thing, said Mistress Molly Cuddle, this sorrow will not last! You come into my beef boudoir... you come in and snuggle with me, darling... Molly's milk will wash away your dolor... and the dream beef will fill you up with a cheerful disposition!

Cherry drank, but feebly, and immediately soiled the purplest and most splendid of Molly's Persian rugs with spew. A voice whirled up into the ear of Mistress Molly Cuddle then and whispered, No more milk for her. The command could not be contravened. Molly moved her face into her cushions. No more milk for you, she pillow-mumbled.

Cherry next sailed out to the late Ernesto Fortunato's island dude ranch, only to discover that remnants of the Clutch had been there already, eaten all the beef, and did not bother with breeding or restocking. They had long since departed, but left behind a monument of beef bones assembled to resemble their former Mistress, Lady Cherry.

She tucked herself inside that colossal skeleton and spent her remaining years there, supporting her nutrition with marrow bone licking and beach sand slurping. In that time, due to legal neglect, all her vast demesnes—both dream and dirt—were assigned to her Staff by Adverse Possession. Elsewhere in the Universe, an angel bear flew blithely onward.

Fed no longer on the dream beef, her body shrank and trembled and finally stilled.

One day, a royal person entered, knelt, and tenderly took her into his arms.

You are alone in the world, said King Dust to Queen Cherry, except for me. Only I, only I, only I, only I will keep you company. And he did, he did, he did, he did.

To Logan Zander Smith—
Mon semblable—mon fils—
Live HERE forever—
Forever in peace.

About the Author

Yarrow Paisley lives in Northampton, Massachusetts. He is the author of *I, No Other* (Whiskey Tit), *Mendicant City* (Snuggly Books), and *Furious in the Expanse* (Eibonvale Press).

About the Publisher

Whisk(e)y Tit is committed to restoring degradation and degeneracy to the literary arts. We work with authors who are unwilling to sacrifice intellectual rigor, unrelenting playfulness, and visual beauty in our literary pursuits, often leading to texts that would otherwise be abandoned in today's largely homogenized literary landscape. In a world governed by idiocy, our commitment to these principles is an act of civil service and civil disobedience alike.